What Reviewers Say About

KIM BALDWIN
"*Force of Nature* is filled with nonstop, fast paced action. Tornadoes, raging fire blazes, heroic and daring rescues…Baldwin does a fine job of describing the fast-paced scenes and inspiring the reader to keep on turning the pages." – *L-word.com Literature*

ROSE BEECHAM
"…her characters seem fully capable of walking away from the particulars of whodunit and engaging the reader in other aspects of their lives." – *Lambda Book Report*

GEORGIA BEERS
"Beers weaves a tale of yearning, love, lust, and conflict resolution. She has constructed a believable plot, with strong characters in a charming setting." – *JustAboutWrite*

RONICA BLACK
"*Wild Abandon* tells how these two women come to realize that 'life was too precious to be ruled by…fears, by…demons.' While these two women struggle with their issues, there is some very, very hot sex. If you enjoy complex characters and passionate sex scenes, you'll love *Wild Abandon*." – *MegaScene*

GUN BROOKE
"*Course of Action* is a romance…populated with a host of captivating and amiable characters. The glimpses into the lifestyles of the rich and beautiful people are rather like guilty pleasures…a most satisfying and entertaining reading experience." – *Midwest Book Review*

CATE CULPEPPER
"…an exceptional storyteller who has taken on a very difficult subject …and turned it into a spellbinding novel. As an author, she understands well that fiction can teach us our own history." – *JustAboutWrite*

JANE FLETCHER
"*The Exile and the Sorcerer* is a mesmerizing read, a tour-de-force packed with adventure, ordeals, complex twists and turns, and the internal introspection of appealing characters." – *Midwest Book Review*

JD Glass

"*Punk Like Me*…is different. It is engaging. It is life-affirming. Frankly, it is genius. This is a rare book in that it has a soul; one that is laid bare for all to see." – *JustAboutWrite*

Grace Lennox

"*Chance* is refreshing…Every nuance is powerful and succinct. *Chance* is not a novel about the music industry; it is about a woman discovering herself as she muddles through all the trappings of fame." – *Midwest Book Review*

Lee Lynch

"Lynch, with a dozen novels to her credit dating back to the early days of Naiad Press, has earned her stripes as a writerly elder. She was contributing stories to the lesbian magazine *The Ladder* four decades ago. But this latest is sublimely in tune with the times." – *Q-Syndicate*

JLee Meyer

"*Forever Found*…neatly combines hot sex scenes, humor, engaging characters, and an exciting story." – *MegaScene*

Radclyffe

"…well-plotted…lovely romance…I couldn't turn the pages fast enough!" – Ann Bannon, author of *The Beebo Brinker Chronicles*

Susan Smith

"This disparate duo's lush rush of a romance - which incorporates reincarnation, a grounded transman and his peppy daughter, and the dark moods of a troubled witch - pays wonderful homage to Leslie Feinberg's classic gender-bending novel, *Stone Butch Blues*." – *Q-Syndicate*

Ali Vali

"Rich in character portrayal, *The Devil Inside* by Ali Vali is an unusual, unpredictable, and thought-provoking love story that will have the reader questioning the definition of right and wrong long after she finishes the book." – *JustAboutWrite*

By the Author

Come and Get Me

Heart 2 Heart

Heartland

Visit us at www.boldstrokesbooks.com

HEARTLAND

by
Julie Cannon

2008

ISBN 10: 1-60282-009-0
ISBN 13: 978-1-60282-009-8

This Trade Paperback Original Is Published By
Bold Strokes Books, Inc.
New York, USA

First Edition: March 2008

Credits
Editors: Cindy Cresap and Stacia Seaman
Production Design: Stacia Seaman
Cover Design By Sheri (graphicartist2020@hotmail.com)

Acknowledgments

This was my first time working with Cindy Cresap as my editor, and as with any *first time* I was excited, scared, and nervous at the same time. I didn't know what to expect or even if I was doing it right. Thanks, Cindy, for your patience, comments, suggestions, and hard work to make this story come to life.

Thanks to Barb Shelton for the story idea. Even after all these years I can still remember mucking Sheila's stall in the middle of the Arizona summer.

For the third time, my thanks to Len Barot, and all the unsung (and sometimes unknown) backroom support at BSB. Without you we couldn't do what we love so you can read what you love.

And one last thing. According to the U.S. Department of Health and Human Services, Administration for Children and Families, at the end of 2005 there were over 500,000 children in foster care in the United States. Two years later the number is even more staggering.

Dedication

For Laura—my cowgirl.
I love every remaining inch of you.

CHAPTER ONE

Where in the hell am I? Rachel was lost. She had been driving around in what seemed like circles for the past twenty minutes. The directions had been pretty clear, but it was obvious that she had missed a turn somewhere. The road was narrow, but she pulled off to the side as far as possible and looked at the map again. She had only been paying half attention the entire two-hour drive from Phoenix, her mind ticking off the unchecked items on her to-do list. She had worked practically nonstop for weeks preparing for this long-overdue vacation. She was tired and grouchy and had a splitting headache.

The sound of another vehicle approaching drew Rachel's attention from the wrinkled paper in her lap. She looked up just in time to see a bright red flash round the curve in front of her. She saw the Jeep an instant before the other driver saw her, and their eyes locked in surprise.

"Holy shit!" Shivley exclaimed, spotting the tan sedan stopped on the narrow road. Stomping on the brakes with both feet and grabbing her dog Lucy by the collar all in one motion, she skidded to a stop just inches in front of the car. "Son of a bitch!" She unlatched her seat belt and vaulted out of the Jeep, Lucy following after her.

Not waiting for the dust to clear, she said, "What in the hell do you think you're doing stopped in the middle of the road like that? You could have got yourself killed, or worse— you could have killed somebody else with your foolishness!" She stopped her ranting when the other driver stepped out of the car and onto the hard dirt road.

Shivley's eyes blazed a trail up from a pair of well-worn work boots to long, slim legs covered by a pair of faded jeans buttoned over a flat stomach. She lingered too long on perfectly formed breasts covered by a thin white tank top. A smooth brown neck led to a pair of very kissable lips partially hidden by golden hair blowing in the breeze. Crystal clear blue eyes stared back at her.

"Oh my God! Are you all right?" the woman said. "I think I'm lost and I was looking at my map again to get my bearings. I pulled off to the side as far as I could. I hadn't seen anybody on this road since the highway and I didn't expect to run into anyone. I'm sorry if I frightened you."

When the woman finally stopped to take a breath Shivley knew she needed to say something, but her voice froze somewhere in her throat. She realized she was standing there with her mouth gaping open but was helpless to do anything about it. The dog sitting attentively by her side began to growl.

"Lucy, quiet," Shivley was finally able to croak out. The Queensland heeler immediately quieted down and sat patiently at her side. Shivley's heart was still racing from the adrenaline of almost hitting the car or worse if she had swerved. There was no guardrail on the dirt road, and the drop to the left was steep and rocky.

"Are you going to speak to me or just stand there and look

at me like I just fell out of the sky?" the woman asked with her hands on her hips.

Jeez, Shivley, get a grip. "I—I'm sorry," she stammered out of politeness. "I guess you just caught me off guard." Her mouth was dry, and her voice didn't sound like hers at all. She cleared her throat and swallowed a few times. "I'm all right. I was just surprised to round the corner and find you sitting here." Shivley was not sure if she was making coherent conversation or not. She'd been overwhelmed by the woman the instant she stepped out of the car. "You said you were lost. What are you trying to find?" Shivley had lived in and around this area most of her adult life and knew most of the roads and landmarks.

"Let me get my map," the woman replied, turning and walking back to the rental car. When she leaned through the open window to grab the map, Shivley moaned at the perfectly round ass encased in tight jeans that fit her like a second skin. The way she walked and carried herself, Shivley came to the conclusion that this was not a city girl. "Snap out of it, Shivley. You act as if you've never seen a woman before," she mumbled to herself when the woman backed out of the car window and headed her way.

"I'm looking for forest road number 23A. I'm usually very good with directions, but I have no idea where I am or how to get there, and my friends are probably worried about me by now." She frowned as she held the map out and indicated where she thought she was.

When she pointed to a place on the map, Shivley noticed that she wasn't wearing a wedding ring, nor was there any evidence that one had ever been there. The scent of perfume drifted to her in the light breeze, and she found it difficult to concentrate. She took a small step back to focus on the conversation and familiarize herself with the map. "You passed it. It's about a mile back on this same road we're on now. It's narrower than this one, so it's no wonder you missed it. If you don't know where it is, you might never find it."

"I'm glad to hear that. I'm pretty good with maps and directions, but I was starting to feel a little stupid because I couldn't find it."

"I can imagine." *Boy, can I ever imagine.* Shivley quickly shut down that thought. She had work to do, and thoughts as pleasant as the ones that were flashing through her mind were distracting. In two days she would be responsible for ten women, and she had to keep her mind clear. She told herself she had no time for diversions, but her mind had other ideas that were transmitted to very specific parts of her body. Her heart had ceased its insistent drumming only slightly, but she remained acutely aware of the beautiful woman standing in front of her.

The ensuing silence was a bit awkward, and Rachel struggled with something to say to prolong the conversation. She didn't know why she wanted it to continue. It wasn't as if she was going to be around to get to know this woman. Hell, she wasn't even going to be around long enough to have an affair with her unless she wanted to fuck right here and now in the dirt. *Hey, now that's an idea.*

For the first time, Rachel took a good look at the driver of the vehicle that had come inches from crashing into her. She was taller than Rachel's own five foot seven by at least three or four inches. She had thick, curly hair that was so brown it gleamed in the midday sun. Her hands looked strong and powerful, and her short-sleeve shirt clearly displayed the muscles underneath her tanned skin. Long, muscular legs a shade lighter than her arms snaked out from beneath a pair of khaki cargo shorts. The words "strong" and "powerful" immediately came to mind. Rachel's headache disappeared and goose bumps rose on her arms. Eyes as black as coal returned her gaze with a twinkle that told Rachel she had been caught looking. *Oops, busted. Good God, Rachel, you really do need to get laid soon.*

"Well, I guess I'd better be getting along, then." Rachel's comment sounded halfhearted.

"I suppose so." Shivley didn't want her to go but knew it was ridiculous to try to stop her. "Back that way about a mile," she reiterated and pointed for emphasis. She held the paper out to the other woman.

"Thanks, I appreciate it." Rachel took the map and their fingers lightly grazed each other.

Shivley glanced at her hand where the woman had inadvertently touched her. It looked perfectly normal, but the spot where they had touched felt like it had just been scorched with a hot poker. Shivley quickly rubbed it several times and took a deep breath.

"Come on, Lucy, let's go." The dog sprang to life at her command, eager to be on the way.

"Thanks again for your help," Rachel added, not knowing what else to say. She carefully turned her rental car around on the narrow road and waited for the Jeep to pass. There was something about the woman that was intriguing, but Rachel couldn't quite put her finger on it. She seethed sensuality in an understated way almost to the point of not having a clue of its effect. She was definitely a lesbian and far different from the women Rachel was typically attracted to. They were hot, they knew it, and they used it to their advantage every chance they had. This was refreshing, if only for a few minutes.

Shivley passed the tan sedan, and a vague sense of loss came over her. She had been drawn to the driver in a way she had neither expected nor experienced in several years. She was so absorbed in her work that she rarely took time for herself and only came into town to pick up supplies. Her social skills—no, correct that—her *flirting* skills had atrophied due to lack of use, and Shivley frowned as she wondered why that suddenly bothered her.

CHAPTER TWO

Tearing open the bag of dog treats, Shivley exited the pet store and stepped onto the sidewalk. Summer had finally arrived, and the warm sun that melted over her body felt glorious. It had been a long winter with above-average snowfall, and she felt every degree below freezing in her bones. The forecast for the last week in May was sunny with daytime temperatures in the mid-seventies. Lost in thought, Shivley turned to walk to the hardware store and ran right into a pedestrian walking in the opposite direction.

"I'm so sorry," Shivley said, automatically reaching out and grabbing the arm of the person stumbling backward. In an instant Shivley recognized her as the stunning woman she'd met earlier in the day. "I guess it's my turn to ask if you're all right." *And if you'd like to have dinner, or go to a movie. Maybe spend several hours in bed?*

"I'm fine, thanks." Rachel returned the smile. "It seems as though we're destined to keep running into each other today."

"It appears so." Shivley glanced up and down to assure herself that the poor woman she had collided with was not injured.

"I'm Rachel Stanton." Rachel held out her hand in greeting.

"Shivley McCoy." Shivley stammered for a moment, not remembering her own name. For the second time that day her mind was completely blank as to what to say next. She never had this much trouble talking to someone, particularly a gorgeous woman. Lucy wiggled at her side and nudged Shivley as if to say, "Hey, what about me?" "Oh, and this is Lucy. She'd never forgive me if I didn't introduce her."

Rachel kneeled down and scratched the dog under her chin. "Hey, girl, nice to meet you too."

Shivley watched in amusement as Lucy nuzzled Rachel's hand and wagged her tail. Dogs and babies were great babe magnets. Not that she was looking for a babe now, but if and when she was, she was confident Lucy would not let her down.

"She's beautiful."

"Shh, don't say that too loud. She has a tendency to get a big head when people give her too many compliments." Shivley smiled and rubbed the top of Lucy's head. Rachel laughed, and Shivley thought she had never heard a more beautiful sound. It was deep and rolling like a bubbling brook and it flowed through her veins.

Rachel stood, or tried to before her right knee buckled. Shivley caught her hand to steady her before she collapsed in a heap on the ground. When she helped her up, she was met with another dazzling smile.

"Thanks." Rachel gingerly applied weight to the affected leg.

Rachel's hand was still wrapped in hers, and Shivley wanted to hold on forever. Her crotch started to beat in time with the blood running a race in her body. She suspected her eyes were giving her away, and to her surprise, she didn't care.

"May I come to your aid again, or do you know where you're going?" When Rachel didn't answer, Shivley reluctantly released her grasp.

"As a matter of fact, I'm going to the grocery store." Rachel pointed to the supermarket on the corner. "It helps that it has a big sign for tourists like me."

Shivley smiled at Rachel's self-deprecating humor. "Where are you visiting from?" *How long are you going to be here? Can I see you again?*

"Atlanta." The place that Rachel had lived for the last few years was just that—a place to live. As a child Rachel had lived in so many different places she never really considered any of them "home." That nomadic practice continued into her adult years, and now Atlanta was simply a convenient place to fly in and out of.

Shivley cocked her head as if to listen a little better. "You don't sound like you're from Atlanta."

"I'm not. I'm a transplant. I confess that at times I can conjure up a soft Southern drawl." Rachel used the last statement to demonstrate.

Shivley's body exploded in sensation, and she thought she might faint. Rachel had done an excellent job of mimicking a Southern woman both in drawl and in batting her eyes coquettishly. It was all Shivley could do not to swoon. She snapped out of her stupor when Lucy nudged her leg. "Did you find your friend's house?"

"Yes, I did, thanks to your directions. I don't think I would have found it without your help."

"Just being neighborly." A vision flashed in her mind of Rachel clad only in a skimpy housecoat standing on her doorstep asking to borrow a cup of sugar.

Rachel focused on Shivley's mouth, and Shivley was unaware of anything other than Rachel looking at her. Rachel licked her lips, and Shivley was entranced by the pink tongue. Her stomach jumped into her throat when Rachel's gaze burned a trail up and down her neck, and she had to fight the urge to throw her head back to allow Rachel greater access.

Rachel shifted and Shivley saw the pulse in Rachel's neck beating in tandem with her own. This was the first sign that Rachel was attracted to her. Shivley could almost taste the salt on Rachel's skin and feel the heat beneath her tongue. She clenched her fists to keep from reaching out and taking Rachel in her arms. Pulling herself together, she stepped back half a step. She wanted to ask Rachel how long she would be in town, but before she had the chance, Rachel spoke.

"Well, I don't want to keep you any longer. I guess I'd better get to the store. Thanks again for all of your help." Rachel stepped around Shivley and her dog.

Shivley nodded and smiled. "My pleasure." And it had definitely been a pleasure. Rachel's eyes darkened, confirming that the suggestive wording of Shivley's acknowledgment was not lost on her before she walked away.

CHAPTER THREE

S hivley woke early to birds chirping outside her window. Stretching her arms and legs and filling most of the king-size bed, she buried under the covers for just a few more minutes of slumber. Lucy, however, had other ideas, and she maneuvered her wet nose under the blanket.

"You know you're not supposed to be up here, young lady," Shivley scolded her but couldn't keep the smile from spreading over her face. She was rewarded with Lucy's long tail thumping against the nightstand. "Okay, I hear you. I'm up, I'm up." Shivley dashed to the bathroom, pulling on her thick terry-cloth robe as she went. When she emerged, she opened the patio door, let Lucy outside, and went into the kitchen to put the coffee on to brew.

After adding a touch of cinnamon to a large mug of steaming coffee, Shivley headed out to the back porch. She loved this time of the day. The sounds of the early morning filled her with strength and peace as she gazed out over her land.

Four years ago she had bought fifteen hundred acres of ponderosa pine after her lover lost her battle with cancer. She and Dale had met while standing in the supermarket checkout line, and after paying for their groceries, spent the next three hours at the coffee shop next door. After they'd been dating for a year, Shivley gave notice on her apartment and moved into Dale's condo. The following year they bought a house, got a puppy, and opened a joint checking account.

Their plan to live happily ever after was completely dismantled when they learned of Dale's illness. At that time Shivley was the owner of an accounting firm and Dale taught third grade in the Flagstaff public school system. Shivley turned the running of the firm over to her most qualified employee and devoted herself to Dale's care. During the last few months of her life, Dale had been in and out of hospitals and hospice care, with Shivley constantly at her side. In the beginning, friends would stop by often, but as Dale's condition worsened the visits became fewer and farther between. Only a handful of friends remained and were close by when she died.

The ranch was Shivley's dream. She had it all worked out in her head. How many acres she wanted to have, the stock she wanted to run, and she had even gone so far as to design the house. It was her dream, not Dale's. Sure, Dale listened while she talked and said the appropriate supportive phrases, but deep down Shivley knew she was just humoring her, and that hurt.

Her thirty-sixth birthday was when she'd first mentioned her ranch, as she called it, to Dale. Her business was thriving, Dale loved teaching, and they had money to spare. They went on vacations, bought the standard lesbian toys, and made the obligatory visits to parents and in-laws. Dale hadn't understood and kept referring to the ranch as her midlife crisis, but Shivley knew it was something more profound than wanting to relive her lost youth.

When she was growing up Shivley wanted to be a cowboy,

even after her father told her little girls grew up to be young ladies, not cowboys. She hadn't listened to him then and she didn't listen to him now when he voiced his opinion of her, her lifestyle, and her choice of residence. Her mother took her vows to love, honor, and obey to the extreme and never once contradicted him in Shivley's presence. Shivley doubted she ever did. Her mother had said little, but her father was appalled when she told him she was selling her accounting practice and her house and using the proceeds and Dale's life insurance to buy land and open a dude ranch. Long ago she had ceased to care what he thought, and even though he and her mother lived only twenty miles from where she was sitting right now, she had never invited him out to see the place.

After Dale's death Shivley lost herself in the ranch, often working until she dropped into bed exhausted. This grueling pace had continued for six months before her best friend Ann came to the ranch and rescued her from herself. Ann had taken over the responsibility of everything inside the house and saw to it that Shivley ate regular meals, went to bed at a decent hour, and relaxed for at least an hour each day. She still worked hard, but in the past few months had started to enjoy life again. It was during one of those quiet times when she happened to mention to Ann her idea of opening a dude ranch. She had enough money to last her a few years if she was careful, but she also knew how unexpected expenses were usually the most expensive. She knew that there were other little girls who dreamed of riding horses, roping cows, and bedding down on the ground under the stars. Well, maybe not directly on the ground, but definitely under the stars. And she thought she could make money at it as well. She named the ranch Springdale in honor of the first spring after Dale's death.

Shivley refilled her mug and returned to the deck. She

put her feet up on the small table, leaned back, and closed her eyes, enjoying the scent and sounds of the forest. Her land held a thick population of ponderosa pine with a sprinkling of aspen trees. She loved the change of seasons, especially when the aspens exploded in color in the fall and wildflowers eagerly popped their heads out of the ground at the first sign of spring.

With a mix of reluctance and anticipation, Shivley stood. "Lucy! Come on, girl." The two almost collided as the dog rounded the corner at full speed. "We have to get ready. We've got guests coming this afternoon, and you know what that means."

Lucy looked at her as if she understood every word Shivley was saying. Her tail wagged so hard the entire half of her body moved with excitement, and she could hardly keep still.

"That's right. Women!"

❖

Rachel looked at her watch as she pulled into the space designated for the return of her rental car. It was odd to see the Timex Indiglo on her wrist where her sleek Cartier watch typically rested. She was far more comfortable with the multifunctional timepiece than with the ever-present showpiece. She was thirty minutes early, and as far as she could tell, the first one here for her twelve fifteen flight.

She turned off the car and leaned her head back. She was tired and her eyes hurt. She had slept fitfully the night before, her dreams filled with a knight in shining armor with piercing black eyes. Rachel was the damsel in distress, and her savior rode in a red Jeep and rescued her. Following the fairy-tale plot line, she rewarded her knight with the proverbial thank-you kiss. It was what happened after the kiss that woke Rachel on the brink of orgasm. She could only remember one other time when a dream was so vivid that she climaxed in her sleep, and the erotic images ticking inside her subconscious last night came very close to doing the same. As it was, she finally gave up on going back to sleep until she took matters into her own hands.

A familiar sound roused Rachel from her partial slumber. She craned her head and saw a plane taxiing into the small airport. Rachel had been on enough private planes lately to recognize this one was a Beechcraft King Air 350, and it was a beauty. The King Air was fully appointed, and Rachel was curious who owned such an exquisite aircraft. She was surprised when an ordinary-looking man and woman descended the steps. In her experience, people who either owned or flew in private jets typically were not shy about flaunting their status, and she could spot them from a mile away. These two were very different.

The man was about forty years old with well-worn jeans and boots that probably hadn't seen a shine in years, which was a direct contradiction to the short-cropped hair and physical bearing of a career military officer. The woman was very similar except she was a good six inches taller and fifty pounds heavier than her companion. She too carried a certain air of authority, and Rachel assumed they must be the flight crew. When no one else exited the sleek aircraft, she opened the car door.

The small boarding area quickly filled with the flight crew and ten women. The room was crackling with excitement, anticipation, and just a pinch of fear.

"Good afternoon, ladies. My name is Gail West, and along with my buddy here, Bart Tillman, we'll be your pilots for our short flight to the Springdale Ranch."

Rachel half listened to the safety briefing, imagining

what the next ten days would bring. The plain but informative brochure said that the Springdale was a working ranch, which meant they would have the opportunity to experience a variety of activities that kept the ranch running while enjoying the great outdoors. Chores included fence mending, cattle tagging, giving of inoculations, and the customary cattle drive. A large block fireplace in the bunkhouse was the showcase picture on the inside flap. Each guest would have her own room with all the amenities, and four women in a Jacuzzi were featured on page three. All this and the opportunity to discover muscles you never even knew you had as well as blisters, broken fingernails, the assorted bumps and bruises, and all for the price of $7,500 per person.

The safety briefing complete, she picked up her duffel and headed for adventure. Rachel chuckled. In a plane this size, every seat was a window seat and every seat an aisle seat, which suited her because she was not in the mood to socialize with her fellow passengers, at least not yet. She had enough of people, talking, and posturing to fill her needs for the next several months. She wanted—no, she *needed* to be alone with no crises, worries, or intellectual challenges to clog her mind.

Rachel was one of the top political strategists in the country and highly sought after by candidates all over the country for her success at getting her clients elected. Lately those responsibilities had morphed into public relations more than anything else. Rachel instructed her candidates on how to walk and stand with an air of authority and confidence, on the amount of pressure they needed in their handshake, and on dozens of other little mannerisms that would magically transform their image into that of a leader. And then there was the spin. The twisting of unpopular positions, politically dangerous liaisons, or previous voting records into whatever angle necessary to get elected today. For the last several months the constant nausea from spinning and weaving sound bites threatened to gag her every time she stepped into a campaign headquarters office. She needed to get away, recharge, and if she was lucky, maybe even get laid.

As a teenager, Rachel had spent three years on a ranch in southern Montana, and thanks to her nonexistent father and irresponsible mother, it was just another place in a long line of places that the state referred to as foster homes. They were never "homes" to Rachel, but places where she slept and ate, and in most cases, where people simply tolerated her for $362 a month.

At first she was appalled by the lack of creature comforts, including no television or stereo, in the Stewart house. They didn't even have a microwave. She was intimidated by the desolation of the ranch, and the wide-open space gave her almost a reverse sense of claustrophobia. There was so much space she felt like a speck in the universe. After she'd brooded for a few days, her natural curiosity and independence kicked in, and in no time she was riding horses, shoveling manure, and feeding chickens. She grew to love the outdoors, the challenge of nature, and more importantly, she learned how to be independent and confident and to rely on no one but herself. She learned a sense of responsibility and respect for that which was bigger than she was. The ranch was just what she needed to tame the wild, rebellious teenager she was becoming. But like everything else that had positively shaped her life, that too was taken away when she was moved yet again to another foster home.

A business associate had spent a week at the Springdale and recommended it as the perfect place to unwind and recharge. It was just what Rachel needed to get her feet planted firmly on the ground again. The Springdale catered to the gay and lesbian community and had soon assumed its rightful place next to P-Town, the Michigan Womyn's Music Festival, and the Dinah Shore golf tournament as one of the must-go places for lesbians, which was an added plus.

Rachel closed her eyes, and the face of an angry, yet stunningly attractive woman sneaked into her mind. It was the woman who had literally almost run her over not once, but twice a few days ago. *Shivley, what an interesting name. Shivley McCoy.* Goose bumps rose on Rachel's arms when she remembered her reaction when Shivley jumped out of the Jeep. After she'd gotten over the initial shock, she thought Shivley was hot. When they met the second time on the sidewalk outside the pet shop, her body had instantly reacted to the smile that lit up Shivley's face. Her breath caught when she recognized desire flickering in the dark eyes staring back at her. It had been far too long since a woman looked at her like that, and she was grateful that her body had not forgotten how to respond.

Two of the women sitting behind her on the plane laughed, and Rachel opened her eyes, glancing at her watch. This time when the women laughed it was the intimate laugh of women in love. Rachel thought about Shivley and wondered for a moment how something as simple as the touch of a complete stranger's hand could make her feel this way. No matter how busy she was, she was always able to find a way to spend some "quality" time with a beautiful woman, but her reaction to Shivley had both confused and thrilled her. But it really didn't matter. She was here and Shivley was wherever butch cowgirls went in this area.

It wasn't long before the plane began descending. The forest was so dense, in some places Rachel couldn't see the ground below. In others, green pasture speckled the ground as if large stands of trees had been cut down for just that purpose. The plane banked to the left and a bunkhouse came into view.

That's a bunkhouse? Even from this distance the house was a sprawling masterpiece of wood and glass that surprisingly didn't look out of place on the pristine land. Horse pens, trucks, and a tractor or two dotted the landscape surrounding the house. A red Jeep was headed toward the landing strip, a soft plume of dust following. Within minutes they landed softly on a dirt runway and coasted to a stop not far from what Rachel suspected was the barn.

❖

A shadow of the plane eerily crossed the field minutes before landing, offering Shivley the opportunity to check her reflection in the rearview mirror. She looked tired, the dark circles under her eyes clear proof she had not slept well the night before. She had tossed and turned, her subconscious dedicated to dreams of the svelte woman she had run into several days ago. Each dream was more vivid than the last, giving her the opportunity to gaze into intense eyes and listen to a soft, sexy voice. The plane pulled in, capturing Shivley's attention, and within minutes both engines had shut down and Bart was at the bottom of the landing stairs. She stepped out of the Jeep to greet her guests.

Shivley evaluated each guest when they arrived. She looked for any natural athleticism, and whether their skin was tanned, either from the sun or a tanning booth. The way they came off the plane and down the steps was an indication of whether they were generally tentative or aggressive in nature. Even the condition of the clothes they were wearing indicated their ability to withstand the rigors of working outside and riding a horse all day. Stiff, dark blue jeans were the first indication that they had been bought specifically for the week. On the other hand, if faded, worn, and slightly tattered jeans could talk, they would say their owners wore them often and kept them busy.

Shivley had carefully selected her stock to accommodate the various skill levels of her guests. Several of her horses were calm and could not be ruffled by anything their riders did. The black gelding was so good that he knew what to do regardless of what his inexperienced rider commanded. She had three or four quarter horses that were for the more experienced riders.

The first woman off the plane was short and stocky, and even from where Shivley stood she could see the large, tight muscles of a bodybuilder. She walked down the steps with an attitude that said she took the world by the balls and would kick anyone's ass who tried to stop her. Shivley filed that away for future reference.

Next out the door was a tall brunette dressed in tight designer jeans, high-heeled boots, and a leather jacket. She looked totally out of place, and Shivley immediately decided to give this fashion plate one of the tamest horses. Her decision was the total opposite when the next two stepped out of the plane. *They could be sisters*, she thought. They were both tall and tan and literally bounced down the stairs. They looked exactly alike except for the length of their blond hair. Following them was a woman who could be no more than five feet tall even in the boots she was wearing.

A casually dressed redhead was after that, and she was holding hands with a woman at least six inches shorter than she. They both stopped at the top of the stairs and took in their surroundings like they were memorizing every detail to recount to their friends at a party after they returned. A woman wearing worn jeans and Dingo boots was crowding the doorway behind them. Her hair was dark and full, and the sleeves of her flannel shirt were rolled up to her elbows. The woman close on her heels was of average height and weight and was wearing a baseball cap pulled low on her head.

Shivley was debating between two horses for the guest at the bottom of stairs when the final woman stepped out. She was of average height but carried herself as if she were much larger. Her left hand tucked blond hair behind her ear while the right hand secured a hat on her head. Shivley experienced a sense of déjà vu as she watched her descend the steps. The wide brim of the hat hid her face until she reached the ground, and when she lifted her head to view her surroundings, Shivley's breath caught in her throat. *Rachel Stanton.*

Chapter Four

R achel's lungs filled with crisp, clean air as she descended the seven steps from the comfort inside the King Air. Trees were in every direction as far as she could see. Tall, majestic living foliage that had survived everything Mother Nature had thrown at it for decades. There was a hint of pine in the air, along with the scent of horses and fresh hay. It was a smell she remembered from her three years in Montana.

Rachel took in her surroundings as she followed the trail of her companions to where they were gathering near the door leading into the barn. The yard and surrounding area were neat and free of weeds and clutter. Directly in front of her were several pens that she assumed were for horses or could comfortably hold fifty head of cattle. The fence was standard four board and showed no sign of disrepair and appeared to have recently received a new coat of white paint. She was a stickler for little details that indicated care and responsibility, and the condition of the fence spoke of the ranch owner's commitment to keeping the property in top condition for the guests. The stables were to her left, with a double set of swinging doors propped open to display stalls neatly lined up on both sides. Several horses stretched their necks over their stall doors, curious at the sounds of the new arrivals.

The crushed granite under her feet would keep boots from bogging down in the mud or tracking it unnecessarily into the house, which was more stunning from the ground than from the air. Sturdy logs wrapped around its exterior, each interlocked with its perpendicular mate at the corners. It reminded Rachel of a set of Lincoln Logs she played with as a child. Eight smooth beams rose from the ground, providing support for the porch and roof. The stone fireplace shown in the brochure faced east, towering over the shake roof that sported three dormer windows. Large four-pane windows flanked a carved front door that was massive yet welcoming. Several rocking chairs waited expectantly on the front porch. A porch swing hung from an end beam and swayed gently in the light breeze.

Rachel walked across the yard. She wore boots and jeans, but today she sported a green long-sleeve Henley shirt. The hat that she'd so casually donned when she stepped out of the plane was more the style worn by Harrison Ford in the Indiana Jones movies than those worn by John Wayne. Rachel's confident steps faltered when familiar, hot eyes met hers. It took a moment for her to realize that the image that had filled her dreams the night before was standing twenty feet in front of her. Her body signaled recognition of Shivley long before her brain, and she somehow managed to put one foot in front of the other. *Does this mean what I think this means?* Her pulse throbbed between her legs at the thought of spending ten days with Shivley McCoy. Rachel smiled as she slowly closed the last few feet between them.

"We have to stop meeting like this," she said, holding in a grin. Shivley's face was partially hidden by the brim of her cowboy hat, and Rachel hoped that she was just as glad to see her.

"And why is that?" Shivley tipped her head, but not enough for Rachel to see all of her face.

Rachel quirked an eyebrow at the question. Shivley still hadn't moved from her pose leaning casually against the Jeep as if she didn't have a care in the world. "People might talk."

"And what would they say?"

"That we're clearly attracted to each other and can't bear to be apart. Or maybe that we're carrying on a torrid affair and can't keep our hands off each other." Rachel hesitated a moment before adding her final thought. "Or maybe they would say that we just want to fuck each other senseless." Her last sentence finally made Shivley lift her head, fully exposing her face. Rachel's gaze made her feel like she had been pinned against the nearest tree. She had seen that look many times and was never disappointed afterward. She crossed her arms across her chest and went for broke. "You pick."

Shivley's imagination drew a vivid picture of what people might think if they came upon them in a quiet place. She flushed and fought to control her breathing. It would not bode well for Rachel to believe that something would come from her suggestive words. She was a guest and it wasn't going to happen. However, the wordplay was fun, and Shivley had not had fun with a woman in a long time. "You have a vivid imagination." Shivley caught the unmistakable flicker of increased arousal in Rachel's gaze. "I like all of them." Shivley winked and took several steps to her right to address the rest of her guests.

"Good afternoon, ladies. I'm Shivley McCoy, owner of the Springdale Ranch and your host for the next ten days."

CHAPTER FIVE

*O*ur *host?* Rachel's ardor soared instantly when she realized that her chances of scoring with Shivley had increased considerably. She wasn't the hired help; she was the boss, and the boss didn't have to worry about losing her job if she slept with one of the guests. The women around her ceased their nervous chatter and gave Shivley their full attention. Rachel watched as each woman introduced herself and Shivley shook their hands. She caught snippets of conversation and was only able to pick up the self-descriptors of doctor, librarian, and mom from a few of her bunk mates. She would learn much more about each woman in the coming days, but the one she wanted to know much, much more about was addressing her now.

"It's a pleasure to see you again, Ms. Stanton. Welcome to the Springdale. I hope you'll enjoy your stay with us. If there's anything you need, please don't hesitate to ask."

Rachel politely took the hand offered to her. It was warm and steady and her body reacted to the contact in the same manner it had the first time they touched. "Thank you, Ms. McCoy. I may take you up on that invitation." Rachel held

Shivley's hand much longer than was necessary. She finally released it when it was apparent that Shivley was growing uncomfortable.

"Please call me Shivley." She turned and addressed her request to the group. "Let me introduce the rest of the staff and then we'll go inside and you can get settled."

Rachel half listened to the introductions, her attention on who was issuing them instead. She was anything but inexperienced when it came to the art of seduction, and as she watched the subtle movements of her host, she planned her next move.

Introductions complete, the guests followed Shivley into the house like ducklings in a neat little row. Shivley stopped in the center of the largest room in the house. "I'll give you a quick lay of the land here in the house and then show each of you to your room. We'll take a tour of the grounds later this afternoon." She spread her arms proudly. "This is the great room." A smattering of laughter interrupted her. "Yeah, I know, kind of self-explanatory, isn't it?"

Rachel estimated that the room had to be at least fifty feet on each side. The interior walls mirrored the outside, the deep grain in the logs intensified by the rustic fixtures strategically located around the expansive room. The furniture consisted of two couches flanked by large recliners inviting their occupants to nap. A large thick area rug filled the center of the room, and lamps sat prominently atop large wooden end tables. Several pillows were scattered around the floor, each more colorful than the one next to it. A large stone fireplace dominated one wall, and two wooden rockers faced the hearth like a bride and groom standing in front of the altar. For such a large room it had a cozy, comfortable feel to it.

Shivley completed the tour of the first floor and everyone picked up their suitcases and headed up the polished stairs.

Rachel watched with interest as two of the women could barely get themselves and their luggage up the fifteen steps to the second floor. She wondered what they were thinking when they booked ten days at a working dude ranch when they were so obviously out of shape. She bet herself a thousand dollars that they wouldn't be able to lift the weight of their bodies into the saddle. The physical requirements of the ranch were such that the unprepared would feel the effects long after they went home. Rachel was grateful that she regularly worked out in any gym she could find while on the road, and she maintained a steady routine of running three miles at least five times a week, rain or shine. Even with her level of exercise, she knew she would be exhausted and sore, and she looked forward to it.

The long hall held six bedrooms, each with its own private bath. Rachel stood patiently while Shivley showed each guest the nuances and features of her room. Finally it was her turn. Shivley opened a door at the far end of the hall, motioning her inside. She intentionally brushed against Shivley when she crossed the threshold. She sensed more than felt Shivley respond and hid a grin that threatened to spread across her face. The future was looking brighter. She stopped a few steps inside and looked around.

The room was warm and inviting, dominated by a four-poster king-size bed covered with a patterned quilt of red and brown with a dark green border. A tan throw was draped over one end while six large pillows lay neatly arranged against the headboard. A nightstand stood on each side and a cedar chest snuggled against the footboard. A dresser with accompanying mirror filled one wall, while the closet and the door to the bathroom lined the other. The walls, painted light brown, were decorated with several oil paintings of ranch life. Several throw rugs would mute any noise coming from the room and keep warm feet off the cold wooden floor. Rachel was exhausted and wanted to lose herself in the thick blankets. She dropped her hat and duffel bag and turned to face her host.

Shivley watched Rachel's reaction to her accommodations. She was impressed that she carried only one bag. Her other guests had at least two, and some even had three. For some reason, it mattered to Shivley that Rachel was comfortable in her home, and she'd surprised herself earlier when she mentally changed the room that she had originally assigned to her. She refused to admit that it had anything to do with the fact that her own room was right across the hall.

"I hope this meets with your approval?"

Rachel took a long, slow look at Shivley's entire body. Her eyes lingered over the important parts, and she could swear she saw Shivley's nipples harden in response. Suddenly she was no longer tired but was filled with mischievous energy. "Where is your room?"

If Shivley had any doubt of Rachel's interest in her, Rachel's slow, seductive perusal of her body erased it. The room was suddenly very small, and the sight of Rachel standing next to the bed was unsettling. Shivley clenched her jaw to maintain control over her mind because her body was rapidly losing it. The only thing that saved her was that she thought Rachel's seduction was too practiced, too perfect to be only for her. Shivley knew that a woman as beautiful as the one looking at her with such undisguised desire rarely slept alone.

Shivley finally answered. "Across the hall."

Rachel's pupils dilated and her chin lifted slightly before she coolly smiled. "Then it definitely meets with my approval."

Rachel's comment was not lost on Shivley, but she chose to ignore it. She knew she needed to leave the room before she did something she might not be ready for, or worse yet, something she was.

"Good." Shivley slipped back into her professional mode. "Come back down anytime. Dinner is at six."

CHAPTER SIX

Shivley was in the kitchen helping Ann prepare dinner. Ann was in charge of the house, and as a matter of practice she and Shivley reviewed the preregistration cards required from each guest, noting any food preferences, allergies, or specific requests for accommodations. Shivley described each woman, helping Ann put the right face to each registered name.

"Okay," Ann said. "So Sue and Cindy are best friends? Jeez, they look so much alike they could be twins. And Christina is the ballbuster?"

Shivley nodded, trying to maintain a neutral expression.

"The redhead and the soccer mom are Becky and Ellen." Ann glanced at Shivley for confirmation before continuing. "Debra's got dark hair and Dingo boots, and Jane always wears that baseball cap."

Again Shivley nodded.

"And finally," Ann said, "we have the contradictions. Joyce the Napoleonic power broker, and Jackie the feminist who wears all designer clothes."

Shivley couldn't help but laugh at Ann's conclusions, but

she hesitated when she came to her description of the guest in the room at the end of the hall.

"Shivley?" Ann asked when Shivley stopped cutting the carrots in mid-slice.

The sound of her name brought her back to the present. "Sorry. I finally figured out why Rachel Stanton is so familiar to me." Ever since Shivley had practically run over the poor woman not once but twice, she had a nagging sense that they had met somewhere before. She would have remembered a woman as beautiful as Rachel, and finally the pieces fell into place. Ann looked at her expectantly. "Her name. It's her name that was familiar. I knew she was going to be a guest here, and I didn't put the two together until now."

"What in the world are you talking about?"

Shivley hadn't shared with her housekeeper how she and Rachel had met, and she quickly filled her in. She had just finished her story when conversation in the great room indicated that the women were making their way downstairs. She handed Ann the knife and joined them.

Throughout the evening Shivley assumed the role of host, bartender, and at times referee. The women were an interesting combination, none of them shy about voicing their opinion on everything from canasta to world hunger. They were all around the same age, but that was where the similarities ended. Debra was a pediatrician and her partner Jane a librarian. Christina owned several Harley dealerships in Las Vegas and Texas. Joyce was a financial adviser, and Sue and Cindy were best friends teaching in the New York public school system. Jackie, a professor of women's studies at Smith College, dominated the conversation, and Shivley worried that she and Jane would come to blows over the apple pie. Thankfully Becky, who was a therapist, and Ellen, a stay-at-home mom, had been together for eighteen years and were able to defuse the situation before anything other than passionate opinions were shared.

Shivley had trouble figuring out Rachel. She had seated herself directly across from Shivley at the table and was now draped across the high-backed chair next to her. Her foot swung back and forth, reminding Shivley of a child sitting in a grown-up chair. She had been the quietest one at the table for the thirty minutes they had been relaxing in the great room with their after-dinner drinks. Shivley's curiosity won out over her patience for someone to ask the question.

"Rachel, we've heard from all the other nine-to-fivers. Now it's your turn. What is it that you do?" Shivley chuckled, suspecting that Rachel didn't have a nine-to-five job.

"A little of this and a little of that," Rachel answered evasively. She refrained from volunteering her chosen profession because it always stirred things up, sometimes to the point of confrontation. She usually said she worked for the government, which more often than not garnered the desired disinterest.

"What the hell does that mean?" Christina asked good-naturedly.

"I know." Ellen piped up. "You're filthy rich, don't need to work, and jaunt around the world spending daddy's money."

Sue added to the guessing game. "No, you're a spy for the CIA and have come here to infiltrate a gang of wild horses." Everyone laughed, including Rachel and Shivley.

Rachel opened her mouth to give her typical response when her eyes met Shivley's. She was looking at her expecting an honest answer, and Rachel didn't want to disappoint her. "I'm a political strategist." Shivley's expression went from polite interest to extreme interest and Rachel was glad she had told the truth.

"What exactly is a political strategist?" Debra asked, refilling her wineglass.

It had been a long time since Rachel had to explain what it was she did, and she thought for a moment. *KISS – keep it simple, stupid.* "I work with candidates to get reelected or those first-timers who want to get elected."

The simple answer did not satisfy Shivley's curiosity. "In what respect?"

The other women had dominated the conversation earlier, so Rachel was surprised when Shivley spoke. It was obvious that she had an inquisitive mind and wasn't satisfied with her benign answer. "I figure out what their constituents are looking for and we develop a strategy to give it to them. We work on what they need to say and how they need to say it in order to get their vote."

Jackie moved to the end of her chair and Shivley held her breath.

"You're a spin doctor?" Jackie's question sounded accusatory.

Rachel had been through this before. The fact was the last few campaigns she'd worked on, that was what she had become. In the course of a few short months she had gone from strategizer and policy maker to spin doctor, rearranging the facts to present a specific agenda or position for an incumbent U.S. senator. She had been forced by the campaign chairman to provide day-to-day tactical responses to claims and accusations released by the challenger. She didn't mind until the exchanges became ugly and downright untruthful. It had made her sick to her stomach to have her name associated with such crap.

Rachel decided to inject some humor into the conversation. "No, I leave that to the sleazy guys. I'm more of a big-picture kind of girl." Her comment was successful, as several of the women nodded their understanding.

"I like the CIA story better," said Jane dryly. Everyone in the room roared with laughter.

Shivley looked around the room at the people she fondly referred to as her "charges" and relaxed. It was always hit or miss when total strangers came together for ten days; throw in physical labor like they probably had never experienced before, and the days got longer and tempers got shorter. As she watched the women and spoke with each one, Shivley fine-tuned her evaluation as they revealed more about themselves and each other. She was surprised at how correctly she had pegged each one. She would need to adjust the schedule and work assignments before they began in earnest in the morning.

The person who fascinated her the most was Rachel. Their first meeting on the road gave her the impression that Rachel was not a city girl, and that was verified when Rachel stepped off the plane in her boots, jeans, and fedora. Shivley watched her move with grace that she expected but with an underlying strength that surprised her. Now she had learned that Rachel was an accomplished professional, hobnobbed with politicos, and was a serious power broker. She was a chameleon, which only added to her mystique.

A creature of habit or an occupational hazard, she wasn't certain which, Rachel spent the evening carefully observing the interplay between the women. They displayed the typical lesbian mannerisms, used the typical euphemisms, and spouted the typical political viewpoints. Ellen and Becky were obviously very much in love, were constantly aware of each other, and touched each other with light brushes of their hands. Honest love was not something Rachel had ever seen much of, especially recently. Political wives and the occasional husband were the norm, each wanting their own slice of power, however they got it. The close relationship between Sue and Cindy was obvious, and to her they sounded more like an old married couple than Ellen and Becky.

Because of her nomadic childhood, Rachel didn't make friends easily. She had lived in eight different foster homes by the time she was eleven and had attended seven different schools, three in one year alone. She lost count of the foster sisters and brothers she had during the thirteen years she was the property of the state of Montana. She didn't allow herself to get too close to anyone, anticipating she would soon move to another home and have to try again to fit in. Looking around, Rachel sensed that once again she was the odd girl out. All that aside, Rachel realized that so far she genuinely liked each woman. Well, almost all of them.

Rachel watched Christina cozy up to Shivley. Having made all the moves herself, she knew Christina was on the prowl and had set her sights on their handsome host. Shivley, however, wasn't giving any indication she was aware of the attack. On the contrary, she spread her attention equally between her guests, ensuring each woman was included in the conversation. Christina was sitting closer to Shivley than was necessary on the big couch and used every opportunity to touch Shivley's arm or leg in the course of conversation. Rachel was surprisingly relieved that Shivley had not acknowledged the gestures and surmised that Christina was probably getting frustrated.

But Shivley had noticed and with practiced ease didn't let on. She was not interested in Christina and had to walk a fine line between letting her know and not pissing her off. She was, after all, a paying customer; a young and beautiful one, but a customer nonetheless who could choose to refer other women to the Springdale or just as easily badmouth it to everyone she knew.

Several times Shivley caught Rachel piercing Christina with a look that could probably bring a grown man to his knees. Rachel never made eye contact with Christina, and Shivley wasn't sure what Christina would do if she did. *She'd probably slide her hand farther up my leg and lean into me some more.* Not that Shivley would mind a hand on her leg and a pair of soft breasts pressed against her, but not Christina's. Rachel's reaction was almost comical until Shivley realized that it felt good to have someone angry about the attentions of another woman.

Rachel was angry more with herself than with what Christina was currently doing to their charming host. When Christina started to make her move, Rachel felt something other than the usual challenge to see who could score first. It was a slow burn deep in her gut that had worked its way to the back of her throat, and there it sat. She fought the urge to wring Christina's neck if her hand wandered any farther north on Shivley's leg. She was a smart girl and knew that jealousy was "stuck in her craw," as one of her foster parents used to say. Why else would she be bothered so much that someone else had her hands on the woman she wanted? The next question that crossed her mind was what was she going to do about it? It would be a long ten days if she got this hung up on Christina's attraction to Shivley.

Several women yawned, and Shivley suggested that they all turn in. She briefly explained the schedule for the next few days, and tomorrow would come sooner for some than others. The two couples rose first and bade the others good night, with everyone except Rachel and Christina following closely behind. The sound of solid doors closing above echoed in the now quiet room. Neither Rachel nor Christina had moved, and after a few minutes Shivley stood, and before she left the room, she encouraged her remaining two guests to do the same.

CHAPTER SEVEN

Six o'clock couldn't come fast enough for Shivley, so she decided to rush it and get up even though it was only a little after five. She had not slept much, images of Christina, Rachel, and Dale swimming around in the dreams in her head. She was making love to Dale, like she had hundreds of times before, when the faces of the other two women superimposed themselves over Dale's face. The images disturbed her when she realized that she had continued to make love to the body regardless of whose face was under her. Before Dale had become ill, their sex life had dwindled from passionate to perfunctory. They were to the point that one of them would simply ask if the other wanted to make love and would not be disappointed if the answer was no. Even before Dale died, Shivley could not remember the last time they made love, and now, four years later, only had a vague sense of what it was like. Several times during the night she'd woken up, and when she finally fell back asleep, the dream began again like a movie rewound in her head.

It had been several months since Shivley had dreamed of her partner. After Dale's death Shivley would see her face every time she closed her eyes. She didn't sleep for days, and when she collapsed in exhaustion she was tormented, reliving the final days of Dale's life. She prayed every day for strength and every night for peace. Eventually God answered her prayers and she stopped dreaming of Dale. In fact, she stopped dreaming altogether and even went so far as to no longer be able to recall Dale's face or her laugh or the smell of her skin. At times she couldn't remember what she looked like without looking at her picture. She endured the stages of grief and eventually resumed her normal sleep patterns. Dale popped into her dreams every now and then, leaving her with a vague sense of guilt that she attributed to not doing more for Dale in her last days. Shaking off the image of a three-headed lover, Shivley showered, dressed, and quietly walked down the long hall to the stairs.

After breakfast Shivley led the women to the barn, where she introduced each one to the horse she had selected for her. She discussed the peculiarities of each of their mounts and even went so far as to tell a funny story about each one as well. Rachel was the last to receive her horse assignment, a buckskin, the kind ridden by Ben Cartwright. The horse was aptly named Bonanza.

Rachel took the reins from Shivley and almost vaulted into the saddle. She had spent hundreds of hours on the back of a horse. She thrived in the outdoors with the responsibility of caring for a horse. She had even begun to enjoy living with the Stewart family until they too were jerked out from under her and she was sent to live elsewhere. Those three years had been one of the rare times she was happy during her childhood.

Shivley watched Rachel's expression go from joy to sorrow before a mask of near indifference appeared under the brim of her brown hat. She wondered what her story was. The way Rachel mounted the horse told Shivley that it was not her first, second, or even tenth time in the saddle. Rachel had experience and lots of it, and Shivley was very curious where it came from. She made a mental note to find out.

The women spent the morning getting the feel of their horses before starting work with them the following day. Shivley kept a close eye on each rider, offering helpful tips for the mildly experienced and encouragement for the novices. She was impressed with Rachel's handling of her buckskin and the assistance she provided to the less experienced riders. She sat tall in the saddle, never once slouching like the others, and rode the stirrups like a pro. Experience had taught Shivley that the other women would be stiff and sore that evening, but she doubted that Rachel would feel much of anything.

Rachel could not remember the last time she felt this exhilarated. It was good to be back in the saddle even if it was a poignant reunion; it felt like it was where she belonged. After only a few minutes, the well-trained buckskin was responding to her commands with only the slightest touch of her leg or movement of the reins. The brawny animal beneath her didn't frighten her. She felt in control of her life for the first time in a long time.

Shivley had surprisingly left her alone. Rachel had checked the box on the registration form that signified her level of horsemanship as "some," and she had expected her host to spend time with her, if not out of politeness then out of legal necessity. She was a little pissed at first when she hadn't, but her anger was quickly forgotten and she maneuvered the strong gelding smoothly around the corral. The wind in her face and the warm sun on her back lulled her into a sense of peacefulness that had eluded her for years. She did not hear Shivley approach her from behind.

"You've obviously spent some time on the back of a horse. You're very good."

Rachel smiled and glanced to her right. "Thanks. It's been a long time, but I guess it's just like riding a bike, it comes back to you after a while." She reached down and patted the horse on the neck. "He's a beauty."

Shivley kept one eye on Rachel and the other on the riders in the corral. "He is a good boy. I got him when he was about four. At least that's as best as the vet could tell. I found him starving in an abandoned corral, and after the necessary legalities of trying to find his owner, some rehabilitation, and a lot of love, he's been here ever since." Shivley looked lovingly at the healthy horse, remembering how he looked when she first saw him. "I must admit, I didn't look very hard to find his owner, and the sheriff's office wasn't interested in sending him back even if we did."

"He's marvelous. How could anybody be so cruel to something so beautiful?"

"Unfortunately, it happens all the time. Horses, dogs, kids. Some people are just pure assholes." The expression that flashed across Rachel's face told Shivley she had stepped into something, but she didn't know what. One moment Rachel was glowing and the next she was slumped in the saddle looking defeated. Shivley didn't know what she'd said and certainly didn't know what to say to make it go away.

Rachel loosened the grip on her jaws and took a deep, calming breath. Shivley had meant no harm in her comment and had no idea of her background, and Rachel knew she had to stop reacting this way. Someday. That was what her shrink had been telling her for months. "Yeah," Rachel replied noncommittally and rode Bonanza to the other side of the coral.

The lunch bell rang, and the women dismounted among moans of pain and talk of never being able to sit again. The Springdale had a large Jacuzzi on the back patio, and it would definitely be full tonight. The women hobbled inside and staggered into the kitchen to eat. All except Rachel. Shivley noticed that she was the last to dismount and spent a few moments gently talking to her horse in low, hushed tones, stroking his neck with affection. Shivley wondered what might be in Rachel's history that was eased by the love of a horse.

CHAPTER EIGHT

L ater that afternoon, half of the women were back on
their horses with Shivley in the lead, Lucy trotting
not far ahead. Debra and Jane paired up behind Shivley, then
Christina and Sue, with Rachel bringing up the rear. They
covered mile after mile of flat timberland touring the ranch,
and Shivley was impressed with their stamina. They stopped
beside a small creek running swiftly from runoff melting
high in the mountains above. Leather creaked as the women
dismounted and led their horses to drink. At Shivley's request,
each woman had packed a canteen before they left the corral
and they drank their fill while their horses grazed along the
bank of the stream.

"It's beautiful out here."

Shivley was double-checking her stirrup and didn't hear
Christina approach. She finished tightening the buckle before
she replied. "I'm glad you think so. You should see it in the
winter right after a snowfall."

"Is that an invitation?"

Christina stepped closer and Shivley immediately regretted
her words. How could she have forgotten how Christina had

made her interest known the night before? "I'm sorry, the ranch isn't open for guests during the winter. Nothing really much to do but feed the horses and sit around and watch the fire."

"I bet I could think of lots of things to do, including some in front of the fire."

Jesus, this girl is persistent. Too bad I'm not interested. "I'm sure you could, Christina, but the ranch is still closed." Shivley was polite in her refusal of Christina's advances, but if she didn't get the hint pretty soon Shivley would have to tell her point-blank, and that was something she really didn't want to have to do. She glanced at her watch as a means of escape. "Better get ready. It's time to head back."

Shivley walked her horse back to where the women were resting. She looked at Rachel and immediately thought, *Now that's someone that I could spend the winter in front of the fire with.* It was apparent that Rachel had been watching her exchange with Christina, and Shivley thought she caught a hint of jealousy in her eyes but didn't know Rachel well enough to be certain. She maintained eye contact and asked, "Everything okay?"

"Fine by me. How about with you?" Rachel noticed that Shivley picked up on the inflection in her voice that was meant to tell Shivley she knew what was up with her and Christina. Anger had bubbled its way to the surface when she watched Christina approach Shivley like a tiger stalking her prey. Rachel was too far away to hear what they'd said, but Shivley appeared to be aware she was the quarry. Rachel didn't like it.

"Fine by me as well. Having a good time so far?" Shivley answered, sidestepping the entire issue.

Shaking her head in understanding, Rachel replied, "Yes, I am. It's beautiful out here."

"I'm glad you like it. You should see it in the winter right after a snowfall." So far their conversation mirrored the one Shivley had escaped from with Christina. She knew Rachel was attracted to her, and she waited to see if Rachel would come back with some sort of pick-up line.

Rachel took the high road. "I imagine it's breathtaking. I'll bet it's so quiet you could hear a pin drop."

Shivley detected a longing in Rachel's voice that she had not heard in the short time she had been on the ranch. She glanced at Rachel and noticed that she was looking at the stand of pines as if she could see the snowy image in her mind. Rachel was not simply being polite or humoring her like Dale had. She gave every indication that she would love it here. Shivley felt a stirring to share it with her.

"Everywhere you look, everything is covered in snow. It's like an Ansel Adams photograph. When the wind blows, it pushes the snow into drifts, and it's so soft you can take a step and end up in snow up to your waist. You fill your lungs with air so crisp and clear you think it's the first day God made the earth." Shivley gazed over her land in awe that it was actually hers and she had the opportunity to love it each and every day. She hadn't realized it until she had spent some time on the ranch, but life had been passing her by every day. She was going through the motions of living, including her relationship with Dale, and like most people, she didn't even know it. She had vowed that she would never find herself in that position again.

Rachel watched Shivley's face transform as she talked about the land and the sky. It had been a long time since she had seen anyone so honestly enthralled with anything having to do with nature. The tingling of what she could only describe as renewal filled her chest, and she closed her eyes and took several deep, cleansing breaths. The pure air seeped into Rachel's bloodstream, making her light-headed. She spent most of her time on the campaign trail in big cities, and this was more oxygen than she had been used to breathing in years.

Rachel had never felt for any place what she felt now after only a day on the ranch. Most of the families she lived with were decent people, but she never felt as if she belonged. More times than she could count, she had to defend herself from the unwanted attention of the teenage boys and occasional father in the houses where she was placed. School was never a haven to escape her home life, the kids often ridiculing her as soon as they found out she had no family. She had learned to have eyes in the back of her head and sleep with one eye open. When other children were safe in the arms of their parents and loved unconditionally, Rachel was shuffled from house to house. When other children brought in baby pictures for a school project, Rachel had none. Rachel never went to a mother-daughter tea or danced on top of her father's shoes at the father-daughter dance. She had never been invited to a slumber party or the prom. She was forty-three years old and had not shed a tear since she was six.

As a result, Rachel had matured into what she thought was an extremely self-reliant woman. She was proud of the fact that she was financially independent and didn't need to be a part of a group like other women she knew. She didn't have a best friend, but a series of casual acquaintances she could call at a moment's notice and go to dinner or a movie if she felt like it, which she rarely did. After spending days and nights with politicians and their handlers, Rachel preferred to be alone when she came home, or so she told herself. She seldom felt any personal connection with anything, any place, or anyone.

But being here on the ranch was very different. Rachel felt a gaping hole in her chest that she didn't know existed until she arrived. It wasn't just the luxuries in her apartment, the leather seats in her BMW, or her BlackBerry that were missing. What was missing was everything. Everything that made life worth getting up for every day. Everything that happened that made her imprint on the world something significant; that what she left behind mattered, really mattered. All of the little things that made life complete. And that something was someone to share it with. The realization was profound. She reached out and grabbed a low-hanging branch on a nearby tree to steady herself.

"Are you okay, Rachel?" Shivley asked, noticing Rachel sway into the tree beside her.

Rachel lifted her head, suddenly very tired. She looked out over the clear meadow. "Right now, at this very moment, I'm seeing things that I've never seen before." Her voice shook.

The shift in Rachel's voice told Shivley that she was talking about something more than the view in front of her. Many guests to the Springdale came to get away or clear their head and often left rejuvenated or with a totally different perspective. She wondered which it was for Rachel. "I hope you like what you see."

Shivley's voice was soft, and Rachel turned her head and met warm eyes looking at her. Shivley held her gaze and Rachel could swear they were communicating on a totally different level. Shivley was offering her space to find whatever it was she needed, no questions asked. Very few people in Rachel's life had given her anything without wanting something in return. Yes, Rachel was expected to pull her weight on the ranch, but this was different, very different. Rachel wanted to work, wanted to give. It suddenly felt as if she needed to make a payment on her soul or she would dry up and blow away. But most importantly, she wanted to do it here, at the Springdale Ranch.

Shivley watched the myriad of emotions sweep across Rachel's face. One moment she was subtle and coy, the next slightly jealous, then sad, lonely, fierce, proud, and finally confused. Shivley had never seen anything as beautiful and frightening at the same time. Rachel was scared, she was running from something, or maybe she was running *to* something. Either way, a sense of protectiveness overwhelmed Shivley to the point that she wanted to wrap her arms around Rachel and cocoon her from whatever demons she was facing.

❖

Dinner was a festive affair. The women were excited about their first days on the ranch and talked over each other telling stories, some already exaggerated into tall tales. Ann kept the food coming and their wineglasses filled, and it was after nine when the last dish was empty.

"Didn't I see a Jacuzzi out back?" Debra asked hopefully.

Shivley had wondered who would ask first. The pulsing jets were often the favorite form of relaxation after a day in the saddle or a prelude to a romantic night under the covers. "Yes, there is. It's heated and ready to go. It's big enough for six cozy or eight intimately." Shivley finished the sentence looking directly at Rachel. "Suits are optional." Several pairs of eyes widened in surprise and several lit up with interest. Rachel's expression was the latter.

Ellen practically jumped from her chair. "I'm in. My ass is killing me. Come on, hon."

"Oh God, yes. I spend way too much time in the therapist chair." Becky obediently followed her partner up the stairs.

The table quickly cleared and the women practically fell over each other in their rush to get into the water. Rachel, however, remained in her seat. "Not interested?" Shivley asked.

"Waiting for the rush to clear." Actually, Rachel wasn't much for intimate group gatherings, and sitting in scalding water with seven strangers was definitely not her idea of a good time.

"It might be a while." Shivley sipped the remaining wine in her glass.

"I can wait."

Shivley's heart skipped a beat. There was more than one meaning in Rachel's declaration. Was she waiting for Christina to lose interest, or was she talking about the Jacuzzi? Shivley suspected it was the former. Rachel continued to intrigue her.

"Would you like to sit in the living room?"

"Only if you'll be joining me." Rachel's reply was straightforward and lacked any pretense of anything other than what it was, an invitation for Shivley to spend time with her.

Shivley wanted nothing more than to continue their conversation. However, she did not want to overstep her bounds. Her guests came to the ranch for a variety of reasons and they typically did not include sitting around and visiting with their host. "Are you sure you don't want to be alone?"

"If I wanted to be alone, I wouldn't have asked if you'd join me."

Shivley was appropriately chastised. "I guess you're right. Shall we?" She stood and picked up her wineglass all in one motion. Following Rachel into the other room, Shivley couldn't help but notice the way she filled out her jeans. It was the same admiration she had the first time she saw this view only a few short days ago. Was it just a few days? It seemed like she had known Rachel forever.

Shivley waited until Rachel sat in the rocker beside the fireplace before sitting across from her. It was her way of keeping a safe distance between them, and from the smile on Rachel's face, she knew it, too. Lucy settled at her feet.

Neither woman spoke for several minutes. The revelation Rachel had earlier in the day and the feelings that accompanied it were threatening to knock down her carefully constructed emotional wall at any moment. She'd won the battle this time, knowing that the next time she might not be so lucky. She fell into the normal light banter she had perfected to get through every day.

"So, why a dude ranch?"

Shivley was lost in her own thoughts as she looked at Rachel sitting across from her. The reflection of the flames from the fireplace cast a warm glow on Rachel's face. Her skin was smooth and flawless, and Shivley imagined Rachel's head in her lap as she stroked her soft cheeks. She couldn't remember the last time she and Dale talked before she fell ill. Yes, they spent almost every evening together, usually in the same room, but they rarely talked. They said words, had conversations, but they hadn't really *talked* in a long time. They were comfortable with each other. After four years they knew practically everything about each other, and there was very little excitement in their lives. They were comfortable with their life and their routine and had taken it for granted that it would last forever.

Rachel waited for Shivley to answer her question. It was obvious by the emotions playing out on her face that she was thinking about something that gave her pleasure and pain. Oddly, Rachel wanted to kiss it away. She was astute enough to know that no matter how much she wanted to kiss her, this was not the time. "Shivley?"

Shivley shook the unpleasant image from her mind. The pain that accompanied any memory of Dale was a remnant of the debilitating, chest-crushing pain she'd experienced the first few months after her death. In place now was a mild stab over what should have been. She put on her best hostess face. "I'm sorry. What did you ask?"

"The ranch. How did you get into dude ranching?"

Shivley sipped her wine and sighed, grateful that Rachel pursued her original question and not one more personal. "I've always been a cowgirl at heart, and the opportunity presented itself and I jumped at it." Shivley knew her practiced answer was weak, but it usually satisfied the other curious guests. Not Rachel.

"How long ago was that?" Rachel asked, crossing her legs.

"About four years ago. In some respects I wish I'd been doing this my entire life." Shivley cringed when she realized that even with that one little comment, she had said too much. It didn't take long to confirm her misgiving. Rachel was a pro at recognizing evasion and probed gently.

"And why is that?"

"Lots of reasons, I suppose." Shivley scanned the room she had painstakingly decorated. "I enjoy the outdoors, and the challenge of doing physical things every day makes me feel good. There's always something that needs fixing or painting or feeding, and I like that, being busy. I suppose it might sound kind of corny, but between the fresh air and hard work there's a sense of peace here. I can't imagine being anywhere other than here." When Shivley emerged from the pain of losing Dale, she realized that her last statement was true.

Rachel was envious of the conviction behind Shivley's words. She was no longer excited about going to work every day, and at times she actually hated it. She was looking for something but didn't know what that something was. She hoped that when it did reveal itself, she would recognize it.

"What did you do before this?" Her calm rocking disguised

her excitement to be able to sit and talk with Shivley with no one around to interrupt.

"I was a CPA."

Rachel sputtered on her wine and barely succeeded in keeping it from spewing out her nose. "A CPA? With blue business suits, pantyhose, and a pocket protector?"

Shivley laughed at the apt description of some of her colleagues. "I'm sorry to disappoint you, but I never had a pocket protector."

"Maybe, but I'll bet your legs were stunning." Rachel looked up and down Shivley's jeans-clad legs as if to make a point.

Shivley's breath quickened and her legs burned where Rachel's gaze traveled. She fought to uncross her limbs and remained still. "I was more prone to pants. Pantyhose make me nuts. I hate them." Shivley intended to sound humorous but was too mesmerized by Rachel's obvious appraisal of the rest of her body to succeed.

"Too bad. I'll bet you were drop-dead gorgeous."

"Yeah, well, that was another life. I much prefer jeans and boots." The crackling of the fire matched the flames jumping in Rachel's eyes.

"You're still drop-dead gorgeous even in jeans and boots." *And what would you look like in nothing at all?*

"Rachel, I wasn't fishing for a compliment." Shivley suddenly wondered how the conversation turned from inquisitive to provocative.

"I didn't think you were."

Shivley didn't know whether to continue the light teasing or shut it down entirely. Rachel was entertaining to be around, intelligent, with a quick wit. She was also very good at flirting, and Shivley had fallen under her spell. Rachel continued to look at her as if she were edible, and Shivley had to deliberately refrain from squirming in her chair. The more Rachel looked at her, the more aroused she became to the point that she thought she might embarrass herself if she weren't careful. She had to get out of this situation, and she needed to do it quickly.

"I appreciate that," Shivley replied, rising from her chair to make her escape. "I've got to check on a few things before I call it a night. You might want to turn in as well. Tomorrow's another busy day." Rachel didn't reply right away but continued looking at her as if she could see right through her weak excuse. Shivley was growing uncomfortable with the awkward silence. Finally, Rachel stood as well.

"You're the boss." Rachel finished her drink in one swallow. She slid by Shivley, but not before she said, "And I always do what the boss tells me to."

CHAPTER NINE

Shivley finished her nightly check of the horses and settled into a chair on the front porch, a cup of warm cider in her hands. The night was cool, a soft breeze lowering the temperature another few degrees. This was Shivley's favorite time of day; her guests had fallen into bed exhausted and the house was quiet. She used this time for reflection. Did she accomplish what she set out to do? Did she do what she wanted to do? Did she live life to the fullest today? Shivley leaned back in her chair, her legs stretching out in front of her, her boots propped on a weather-beaten wooden table. Crickets chirped their own form of communication in the darkness, and the livestock were settling down for the night.

Shivley sipped her drink. The first couple of years she would sit on the porch in this exact spot imagining Dale sitting beside her. They would talk about their hopes and dreams for the ranch and their life together. After a while Shivley finally recognized that it was just a dream and Dale would have never been sitting beside her even if they had made the move and bought the property. Actually, it never would have happened in the first place if she had not died.

Shivley was happy here, happier than she ever thought she could be. It took Dale's death to put her in a place where she could spend the rest of her life. Guilt overwhelmed her whenever she thought about it, so she avoided thinking about it.

"May I join you?"

Rachel stepped out onto the porch, pulling Shivley back to the present. "Of course." She sat up, her feet dropping to the porch deck.

Rachel slid a chair closer to Shivley and sat down. She had been watching Shivley for several minutes, debating with herself whether she should interrupt her private time. Shivley looked like she belonged right where she was. Rachel thought that the image in front of her could have been on a postcard or in an episode of *Bonanza*. She didn't want to intrude but had an overwhelming urge to be sitting beside Shivley.

"I thought you turned in?" Shivley glanced at Rachel when she sat down beside her. She usually didn't venture out onto the porch to unwind until her guests had gone to bed. Rachel's interruption was a pleasant surprise.

"Changed my mind," Rachel replied, annoyed that she had given in to the urge to spend more time with Shivley. She had been fighting the need to be with Shivley, to learn more about her ever since they first met on the dirt road. Rachel was not used to this amount of curiosity about another woman. Typically she was interested in them, yes, but generally not more than superficially and certainly not in knowing what made them tick.

"Too quiet?"

"Too excited."

Shivley laughed. "Yeah, that happens. The first night is always full of anticipation, then every other night is sheer exhaustion."

Shivley's laugh flowed through Rachel's veins. "No doubt."

The silence was comfortable. Shivley felt no need to fill the space with chatter to make her guest feel at ease. She glanced over at Rachel, her face lit by the full moon. She looked content. Other guests were nervous, anxious, or outright bored. Rachel appeared to be none of those. The silence stretched on and Shivley thought Rachel had fallen asleep until she spoke quietly.

"I envy you."

"This is pretty damn good, isn't it?" Shivley knew what Rachel was referring to without her needing to spell it out. The outdoors, a ranch, animals, nature, cloudless blue sky with stars so bright you almost had to cover your eyes.

"Is it everything it appears to be?" Rachel knew life was usually anything but.

"For the most part."

"I'll bet the downside is worth it, though."

"You mean the blisters, calluses, sore back, mud, rain, dirt, and blood? Then, yes. It is definitely worth it." Shivley meant every word. Her job now was by far the hardest, most mind-numbing, physically challenging job she had ever had. And she loved every minute of it. She would not trade it for anything in the world. "If you promise not to tell anyone, I'll share a secret with you."

Rachel's interest piqued. "Cross my heart." She mimicked her words with the action.

Shivley looked around, checking to make certain no one else was within hearing range. She took a deep, steadying breath. "When I break a nail, it almost brings me to my knees."

Rachel frowned, confused for a moment, then she laughed. She was joined by Shivley and they both were laughing so hard, tears trickled out of their eyes. Rachel was finally able to take a breath.

"My God, you were so serious I thought you were going to tell me a group of ranch gremlins came in every night and did all the real work."

Shivley was still struggling with her own breathing, not entirely caused by the humor they were sharing. Watching Rachel laugh without a care in the world was what really almost brought her to her knees. After what seemed like forever, she pulled it together. "How could you think such a thing?" she replied in mock disgust. She paused. "They only come twice a week." She was rewarded again with the sound of Rachel's laugh carrying into the night.

CHAPTER TEN

S hivley frowned as her foot hit the last step on the stairs. The light in the kitchen was on, and as she glanced at her watch she saw it was too early for Ann to be preparing breakfast. The thick carpet muffled her boots as she walked across the expansive living room. Not certain what she would find, she peeked around the corner.

Rachel was fast asleep with her head on the table, Lucy curled up at her feet. Shivley scooted her inquisitive pooch away from the sleeping form and out the back door. That task accomplished, she was unsure if she should wake Rachel or let her sleep. She was lying in an awkward position, and Shivley was afraid she would wake with a neck so stiff she wouldn't be able to move.

While she contemplated what she should do, she took the opportunity to silently observe her. Blond hair had fallen across most of Rachel's face, and Shivley was tempted to brush it away but stopped herself before she moved. Muscles that she hadn't noticed before were prominently displayed in arms that were crossed, providing Rachel's head with some cushion against the hard pine of the table. The portion of her face that Shivley could see was pasted in a frown as if she were scowling at the world. Rachel's feet were bare, and Shivley smiled at the toenails, polished bright red, peeking out from under the frayed hems of her jeans.

Even in sleep Rachel was beautiful, and warmth seeped into Shivley's bones. It had been so long since she'd felt warm inside because of a woman. But here she was in the presence of a beautiful, desirable woman who wanted her, and she felt like shit. It was one thing to flirt but another thing altogether to do something about it. She enjoyed the verbal sparring with the women who came to her ranch, knowing it was harmless and that she would never act on it. Until Rachel Stanton stopped her car in the middle of the goddamn road.

She must have made a noise because Rachel's eyelids fluttered open. "I'm sorry. Did I wake you? I was trying to be quiet. Actually, I was trying to decide if I should wake you or let you sleep." Shivley knew she was babbling.

Rachel sat up slowly, stretching her neck as she rose from the table. "Ouch. I just laid my head down for a minute, an hour ago," she said, looking at the clock hanging above the toaster. She rubbed her neck. "I'm getting too old for this." She had tossed and turned most of the night thinking about her host and had finally given up trying to sleep and come downstairs.

She had wandered through each room touching a knickknack here and there, learning more about Shivley. The rooms were not professionally decorated but bore the hand-picked tastes of their decorator, from basic, functional items to classic pieces of western memorabilia. The home of one of Rachel's clients had been featured in *Architectural Digest,* and when she saw it in person it felt cold and impersonal, a museum where nothing was touched, sat in, or walked on. Her client had three young children and there was no evidence of their existence anytime she was at their home. Missing were the finger paintings cluttering the refrigerator door, the clay mug made in third-grade art class, the stray sock lying curled up in the corner. Everything had a place, nothing was out of place, and sadly, Rachel realized her apartment was just like it: a showpiece. Definitely not a home.

Shivley's home, on the other hand, was warm and inviting, and felt lived in. An eclectic array of wooden carvings filled the second shelf of the bookcase, each one bearing the initials "SMC" on the bottom. The impression Rachel had so far of Shivley was that she had none of the pompous pretense of most of the people she knew. They didn't even try to hide it, whereas Shively was everything she appeared to be.

Shivley crossed the kitchen, stood behind Rachel, and began massaging the tight muscles in her neck. "You should go back to bed. It's still an hour until we need to get up and get started."

"If I do, then you'll have to stop what you're doing and I don't want you to. It feels wonderful."

Shivley stopped and quickly lifted her hands from the warm neck. *Oh my God, what am I doing?* She was shocked that she had so casually started rubbing Rachel's neck, as if she'd done it every night for years. She was even more appalled that she had laid her hands on a guest so intimately, something she would never dream of doing. Other than basic first aid and hugs from friends and family, Shivley had not touched a woman since Dale died. She missed the softness of a woman's skin, the way her fingers glided over tight muscles and the curves of hips, the underside of breasts heavy with desire, filling her palm.

The gentle sound of her name floating from Rachel's lips was almost enough to push Shivley over the edge. Her hands were trembling, and if it weren't for the counter she was leaning against, her whole body would have been shaking as well. Rachel's skin was so warm and soft she fought the urge to caress it for the rest of her life. The images in her bizarre dreams instantly came back to her, but the only face she saw this time was Rachel's.

"Shivley?" Rachel said, her voice heavy with concern. "Shivley, what is it? Are you okay? Did I do something wrong?" She rattled off the questions, hardly giving Shivley a chance to answer any of them.

"I'm fine. Really," Shivley added, noting the expression of disbelief on Rachel's face. She wasn't fine, and Rachel standing so close to her was not helping her regain her equilibrium in the slightest. "I'm the one that should be apologizing to you. I never should have done that." Even to her own ears the apology sounded weak.

"Done what?"

Shivley wanted to step away. No, she needed to get away from Rachel, but the pounding of her heart and the throbbing in her crotch was intercepting the command between her brain and her legs. "Rub your neck. I never should have done that."

"Why?" Rachel sat back in her chair and folded her arms across her chest.

"Because you're a guest."

"So?"

"So? So, you're my guest and I shouldn't be touching you like that."

"Why not?" Rachel slowly stood. "What if I wanted you to?" She stepped closer.

Shivley looked at the red lips only inches from hers. "That's not the point." Her voice was barely a whisper.

"What *is* the point?"

Rachel licked her lips, narrowing the space between herself and Shivley until her lips were so close Shivley could almost taste them. Her pulse was in hot pursuit of her heart and it pounded deep in her chest. The lips moved closer and there was no doubt in her mind of Rachel's intentions. She was at a loss to think of any reason to stop her. "The point is that—"

"The point is," Rachel interrupted, "I'm going to kiss you."

The first touch of Rachel's lips took her breath away. The kiss was soft and tentative, as if Rachel were asking permission to continue, not assuming that it would. Rachel released her lips, giving Shivley the chance to break off the kiss. When she didn't protest, Rachel once again covered her mouth, this time more sure of herself. Shivley was aware of nothing but the sensation of soft lips caressing hers. When Rachel's tongue lightly tickled her bottom lip, she shuddered. She hadn't been kissed like this in a long time, and until this moment, she hadn't realized how much she missed it. Shivley shifted from being an observer to an active participant in the experience.

Rachel registered the instant Shivley dropped her defenses, and she drew her into her arms. Shivley did not object; on the contrary, strong arms wound around Rachel's neck and pulled her closer. She took that as an invitation to deepen their kiss, and her tongue entered Shivley's warm, wet mouth. Shivley moaned and Rachel was certain Shivley wouldn't stop her because they both were obviously enjoying the exchange. *God, she can kiss!*

The sound of a throat clearing penetrated the haze of desire that had cloaked Shivley like a warm summer sky. She reacted first and quickly lowered her hands and pulled Rachel's arms from around her waist. She glanced over Rachel's shoulder, hoping it was not one of the women from upstairs. Guilt flooded her when she met the questioning eyes of Ann.

CHAPTER ELEVEN

S hivley untangled herself and shot Rachel an apologetic
look before stepping around her. "Good morning." She
glanced at the clock. "You're up early. I didn't expect you."
Shivley knew how stupid her greeting sounded. She wouldn't
have carried on like this if she expected Ann to walk in at any
moment.

"Obviously. Should I come back later, or would you two
like some coffee?" Ann's expression turned from concerned to
teasing. "Or maybe a cold shower?"

Rachel replied first. "That's not a bad idea." What she
really wanted was to continue kissing Shivley for hours, but
she knew there was zero chance of that happening, at least not
this morning. She turned on her heel, headed for the shower,
and left the two women standing in the middle of the kitchen.

"Don't say it." Shivley raised her hand, palm out.

"I wasn't going to say a word."

"Yes, you were." Shivley knew better and wasn't up to
answering the questions lurking behind Ann's eyes. However,
she didn't have any choice.

"Sit down and tell me about it while I make the coffee." Ann was more than Shivley's housekeeper. They had been friends for more years than Shivley could remember, with no sexual attraction between them to get in the way of anything but a wonderful friendship. Shivley valued Ann's opinion, and the only advice Ann ever gave, Shivley had asked for.

Shivley filled Ann in on the early morning activities, specifically omitting her reaction to Rachel's kisses. She knew Ann would read between the lines and wasn't disappointed.

"I'm pretty sure the answer is yes, but is Rachel the first woman you've kissed since Dale?" Shivley nodded. She didn't count the kiss a few months ago at a party. That was more of an assault than a kiss. "And?"

"And what?" Shivley pretended she didn't know what Ann was asking. The look she received told her Ann didn't believe she was that dense. "It was okay."

"That didn't look like just okay to me."

"All right, it was more than just okay. I liked it."

"That's better. I know it's been a long time, but shouldn't you be glowing and tittering like a schoolgirl?"

Shivley covered her face with both hands as if she could rub away the situation. "I can't do this. Besides the fact that she's a guest, I just can't."

"Why not? I admit it's not the best policy to get involved with a guest, but if she's offering and you're interested, where's the harm?"

Shivley struggled to find the words that would adequately describe the rage of emotions surging through her body since that first moment she saw Rachel on the hard dirt road.

She clearly remembered the first time she had gone out socially after Dale's death. Her friends had nagged her for weeks to come to a party they were having, and she finally gave in to get them off her back. The first thing she remembered was that she didn't have a clue what to wear. Every stitch of clothing she owned was bought to wear on the ranch and didn't seem appropriate for a casual party. She refused to go out and buy something, because then it would be actually acknowledging it was a "social" occasion, and she wasn't ready to "socialize."

Once she got there, she felt like she had stepped into the future. She and Dale had been together four years and she was definitely rusty in small talk. Besides, she was not in the dating game; she was sitting on the bench. The inane conversation with women half her age who had absolutely no idea of challenge, hardship, or even life, for that matter, bored her.

The final straw was when she was talking to a woman who appeared to have it together, when she slowly lowered her head to kiss her. There was plenty of opportunity for Shivley to pull away, but she knew she had to get back in the saddle, so to speak, and she met the woman halfway. The kiss was not unpleasant and she actually enjoyed it until it turned demanding, the woman's hands roaming like she had every right to.

Panic and guilt swept over Shivley, and she pulled away. At least she tried to. The stranger must have thought all she needed was a little more convincing and held her tighter, pinning her to the patio rail. Shivley got her hands between them, pushing on her chest and twisting her mouth away. The woman finally got the clue and turned her loose. Shivley didn't hear the choice words behind her; she was halfway to the front door.

"Shivley?" Ann's question pulled her back to the present.

Shivley had felt something very different for Rachel, a complete stranger, and it had rattled her more than she expected. She knew nothing about Rachel other than she was gorgeous and a fabulous kisser. She shuddered to think Rachel might have a girlfriend stowed away somewhere. She thought otherwise. Someone as smooth in seduction as Rachel would never allow herself to be caught.

"I feel guilty."

"Shivley, it's been four years since Dale died. Did you hear me? Dale died. Not you. You are alive and need to start living. I know you loved Dale and she loved you, but she wouldn't expect you to never find happiness again. She told us as much." Ann's eyes softened with her last words.

Ann was right and Shivley knew it. She and Dale had talked late into the night shortly before she died, and Dale had made it very clear that she did not expect Shivley to remain alone the rest of her life. "That's not it, Ann."

"Then what is it?"

Shivley couldn't describe the thoughts she was having more frequently. One minute she could put her finger on it and the next, it had slipped through and was just out of her grasp. Ann placed another steaming cup of coffee in front of her and sat down across the table.

"Shivley, I'm your best friend and I can tell you this as well as anyone else, but you have to listen to me." Shivley studied her with interest. "Sister, you need to get laid."

Shivley had just sipped her coffee, and Ann's stark words sent the hot liquid down the wrong pipe. She coughed and slapped herself on the chest. Her plight didn't faze Ann in the slightest.

"Yep, a good, old-fashioned, honest-to-goodness fuck. That's what you need." Ann shook her head and wore a satisfied look as if she had just figured out a magician's secret. "The kind that absolutely blows your mind and knocks your socks off. You don't ever want to get out of bed, and when you do, all you can think about is getting back in with the warmest, sexiest woman in the world. The way she touches you…"

Between the heat from Rachel's kisses and Ann's descriptions, Shivley had heard enough. "I get it, Ann."

"Oh, sorry." Ann waved her hand in front of her face, fanning herself. "Maybe I need to take my own advice." She stood. "Guess I'd better get breakfast started. Everyone should be getting up soon."

"Good idea. Get started on something you know something about and stay out of my business," Shivley grumbled with a poorly disguised smile.

Ann nodded her head toward the doorway as she spoke. "It's not me who wants to get into your business."

Shivley knew Rachel was standing behind her without having to turn around. Her pulse quickened and she wondered just how much of their conversation Rachel had overheard. She didn't have to wait long to find out.

Rachel walked into the kitchen and spoke so only Shivley could hear. "She's right, you know. A good fuck does wonders." She continued to the coffeepot, barely breaking stride. Filling her cup, she glanced over her shoulder for Shivley's reaction. Unmasked lust stared back at her. She boldly returned the message. Before their heated exchange could ignite into flames and burn the house down, the remaining boarders stepped into the room, clamoring for coffee and breakfast.

While they ate, Shivley gave the women a briefing of the day's activities. She made eye contact with every woman except Rachel. If she had, images of fucking her, as Ann had so crudely put it, would dance in front of her and she would lose her train of thought and probably turn into a drooling idiot. She labeled it as self-protective behavior and kept her eyes and thoughts away from Rachel Stanton.

The women set out right after breakfast, Shivley leading the way and Lucy trotting excitedly by her side. The sun was at their back, excited chatter from her guests filling the brisk morning air. Shivley had recently purchased the adjacent property, adding an additional four hundred acres to her holdings. As a result, the fence line needed to be extended to surround the new property before she could let her herd graze on the new land. The women would be spending the first part of the day digging holes, setting fence posts, and stringing barbed wire.

Riding out, Shivley spent a few minutes with each woman, ensuring they were all comfortable in the saddle and answering questions. As she rode, she felt eyes watching her. One set she knew belonged to Christina. The woman had made her interest very clear to Shivley again this morning, and Shivley would have to tread lightly so as to not offend her. The other pair of eyes was watching her approach now.

"Doing all right?" Shivley asked, her horse falling into cadence with Rachel's.

"A little stiff, but not nearly as much as some of the others," Rachel replied, nodding at the other woman riding ahead of them.

Shivley smiled, nodding in agreement. "Yeah, Ann handed out quite a few doses of ibuprofen this morning." Rachel was one of the few women she had not given any pain reliever to. Shivley watched Rachel out of the corner of her eye as they rode comfortably along. Rachel knew what she was doing on the back of a horse. She sat tall and comfortable in the saddle, her legs fitting perfectly in the stirrups. She held the reins loosely, worn leather gloves protecting her hands from the elements. Her hat was pulled down low on her head, her hair pulled back in a ponytail. The sleeves of her shirt were rolled up to her elbows, exposing arms already tanned from the sun. The top three buttons of her shirt were open, but her neck was partially hidden under the blue bandana tied casually around her neck. By far Rachel was the most appropriately dressed for the day.

They rode the remaining twenty minutes in silence, and when Gail and Bart dismounted next to a pile of shovels, picks, and an auger, Rachel finally spoke. "Damn, looks like the gremlins had the night off."

Rachel's laughter was still ringing in Shivley's ears when she dismounted and called the other women around.

❖

Directions given and tools handed out, the women broke into teams and began the work for the day. Rachel was in the group with Sue, Cindy, and Joyce, all of whom were from New York so they chatted endlessly about familiar locations. Debra and Jane were with their pilot-turned-ranch hand Gail. Bart was teamed with Christina, Jackie, Ellen, and Becky, and Shivley was the foreman of the job. Shivley suspected that Rachel would know how to set a post, but kept an eye on her group nonetheless. She was not disappointed.

While the rest of the women struggled with their turn with the auger, Rachel and Cindy handled it like seasoned veterans. Both women were tall and strong, a must for controlling the speed and direction of the hole-digging machine. As a matter of fact, several times Shivley found herself staring at Rachel standing with legs spread wide for balance, stripped down to a thin tank top, muscles glistening with sweat. Shivley knew her mouth had probably been hanging open as well.

Once their forth hole was dug, Rachel took her canteen off her saddle horn and sat in the shade of a mesquite bush while Sue and Joyce dug out the loosened dirt with their shovels. As she looked around the group, she spotted Shivley helping Debra and Gail.

Her shirt was off, revealing a well-developed upper body clad only in a short-sleeve white T-shirt, her damp sports bra soaked through the thin fabric. The muscles in her legs strained against her jeans when she lifted the heavy post from the stack into place in the hole. Mission accomplished, she took off her hat and wiped the sweat from her face with her green bandana. Rachel had been with many beautiful women, but none had the natural beauty Shivley was displaying now. It was raw and effortless, unlike the synthetic breasts, manufactured faces, and liposuctioned tummies of the women she associated with. She was suddenly very thirsty and could almost taste the salt on Shivley's skin. Her canteen was halfway to her lips when Shivley turned and looked at her. She froze, her body instantaneously on fire, neither woman breaking the connection.

Rachel could hardly breathe, and it was not from her recent physical exertion. Shivley's eyes devoured her and she felt as if they were the only two people on earth. The sun was shining and the light breeze in the air did nothing to cool her heated skin. She wanted to go to Shivley, to have her hands touch her body the way her eyes were caressing her now. She wanted to make love with her under the clear blue sky with nothing but nature between them. She was parched for connection and Shivley was her beverage of choice.

Shivley heard her name called from somewhere far away, and each time it seemed to be coming closer until she realized Debra was standing right next to her. By the look on Debra's face, she must have called her name several times before it penetrated her lust-filled brain.

When she had turned and saw Rachel watching her, Shivley fell into the vortex of her gaze. It felt as if the world around her was spinning and she and Rachel were standing perfectly still in the center. Shivley literally could not move. She had never seen such yearning, such unmasked desire directed at her. She was both thrilled and frightened by what she saw and didn't know which one to act on first.

"I'm sorry, what did you say?" Shivley was able to stutter. She hoped that her other guests hadn't seen her outright ogle Rachel like she had just been doing.

"I asked if this was deep enough," Debra replied, pointing to the hole they had just dug.

Shivley tore her eyes away from Rachel and tried to focus on the point in question. It took several seconds of concentrated breathing for her to gather her wits to be able to answer.

CHAPTER TWELVE

Just before noon Shivley had everyone mount up and led them back to the stream where they had been the day before. Ann was waiting with lunch and several coolers of cold drinks. Soon the hisses and pops of soda cans peppered the air as the women settled in for their midday meal.

Ann had also brought along six all-terrain vehicles. They were lined up in twos on an aluminum trailer pulled behind one of the pick-up trucks Shivley had on the ranch. The vehicles were all shiny red, with large knobby tires to grab the rough terrain, and metal racks on the front and rear to carry whatever gear was needed. Today, the racks were empty and the gas tanks full.

Jane spoke up first. "Are those for us?"

Shivley had a mouth full of ham sandwich and could only nod.

"Cool, I love riding quads," Christina piped up.

A chorus of "Me too's" followed, and in no time Ann and Shivley had the vehicles unloaded and the wide black vinyl seats occupied. Debra rode with Christina, Ellen and Jane doubled up, with Sue and Cindy going solo. Shivley was helping Ann clean up after lunch when she felt rather than saw someone standing behind her. Her skin prickled and the hair on the back of her neck stood up.

"Will you take me for a ride?"

The request was simple enough, but Rachel said it in such a way that there was no mistaking the double meaning. Shivley cast a quick glance at Ann, who was struggling to hold in an "I told you so" smirk and turned around. Rachel was so close that Shivley's arm brushed across her breasts, and Shivley's eyes got no farther than the nipples that had sprung to attention under the inadvertent brush. She couldn't speak.

Rachel's nipples were hard and her crotch throbbing when she reached for Shivley's hand and led her silently to the empty quad. She climbed onto the rear of the seat and patted the front, indicating she wanted Shivley to drive. Rachel wanted Shivley in front of her where she had unimpeded access to the body that was driving her crazy. Her hands itched to touch Shivley, and this was the perfect opportunity. Shivley slid into the seat, turned the key, and started the powerful engine. Rachel wrapped her arms around her middle and leaned into her. She was inches away from Shivley's ear when she said, just loud enough for Shively to hear, "I'm ready whenever you are."

Spasms shot through Shivley's body in the course of several seconds. First when Rachel put her arms around her, then when she leaned her hard nipples into her back, and finally when her warm breath tickled her ear. Shivley wasn't sure how long she would be able to concentrate on her driving with Rachel in this position. When Rachel's hands drifted lower on her belly and her fingers grazed her crotch, Shivley gunned the throttle and they took off.

It took several seconds for Shivley to regain control of the vehicle and reduce the speed to what was appropriate for the terrain. They rode along the bank of the stream, following the trail the other riders had taken a few minutes ago. Shivley's hands grasped the handles tightly, her knees hugging the warm gas tank. The placement of Rachel's hands was another matter altogether. They roamed freely over her stomach and thighs, and up and down her sides until Shivley almost crawled out of her skin. Rachel had her in a compromising position and was using it to her advantage.

"I like this." Rachel spoke into Shivley's ear.

Rachel's breasts were pressed tightly against her back and her legs straddled her ass, and Shivley groaned out loud. She knew Rachel could not hear her over the noise of the engine, and it gave her a millisecond of relief from the torment Rachel was putting her through. She shifted gears, and when Rachel's hands drifted north, she released the clutch too quickly and the engine sputtered and stalled, coming to a sudden stop.

"Jesus Christ, Rachel, you're gonna get us killed." Actually, Shivley was already dying a slow death from Rachel's teasing.

Rachel's hands were just under the curve of Shivley's full breasts, and when she leaned forward, she could see Shivley's nipples straining against the fabric. Her fingers started to move. "Mmm, I like this a lot." She was almost purring.

Shivley grabbed Rachel's hands before she could do any more damage to her self-control and laid them on her thighs, covering them with her own. "Rachel, I mean it. You can't do that. It's dangerous. Someone could get hurt."

Shivley's tight muscles quivered under her fingers, thrilling Rachel with her response. "You're the one who's dangerous." She squeezed Shivley's legs.

Shivley closed her eyes and begged for strength. "No, you're killing me and you have to stop." Her last few words faded away.

"And if I don't?" Rachel didn't stop, nor did she move

away from the tight embrace. What she did do was nibble on Shivley's exposed neck.

Shivley was rapidly losing the ability to keep her libido in check. Rachel's hands were waking up parts of her body that had been asleep for a long time. Her fingers tingled and her toes started to curl. She needed this and she needed it badly. It shook her to realize that she had never needed Dale as much as she needed Rachel right now. But she was not so far gone that she didn't realize where they were and the ramifications should someone show up at the wrong moment, or any moment, for that matter.

Shivley clenched her teeth. "I'm asking you to." When Rachel still did not move, she added, "Please."

Rachel wasn't about to let her go. She finally had her right where she wanted her and was not going to let any grass grow under her feet. She knew that if she said one word or moved just a fraction closer, Shivley would be hers. She wanted Shivley, needed her, and craved her like she had never craved anyone before. The vibration of the engine and feel of Shivley's hard muscles reacting to her touch had Rachel wound tighter than ever before. All she needed was one simple touch and she would go over the edge. Shivley had not moved away from her, but Rachel detected desperation in her voice and it touched her. She wanted Shivley, her body was screaming for her, but not like this. Rachel had never given a second thought to *persuading* a woman who needed just a little bit more to step over the cliff. But this was no longer just about her and her needs. Shivley had to want her in the same equal way, or it would mean nothing. And Rachel was suddenly tired of nothing.

Rachel dropped her hands to Shivley's waist without saying anything more. She could have teased her some more. She wanted to, but something held her back. They rode back to the group in silence, Rachel hanging on chastely to Shivley's belt loops. Shivley cut the engine and Rachel stepped off, running her hand teasingly along Shivley's tense shoulders.

"Relax, I won't do anything you don't want me to." Rachel turned around and headed for her horse.

❖

On their return to the ranch, Shivley was shadowed by Christina for most of the ride. The only time Christina left her side was when the trail became too narrow for two horses, and she resumed her position as soon as she was able. Shivley kept an eye on Rachel, who rode several lengths behind her, chatting quietly with Jane and Joyce. Several times Shivley heard her laugh, and butterflies danced in her stomach.

Shivley recalled their ride and the feel of Rachel's arms wrapped around her, her warm breath on her neck. She finally admitted that it had felt good, and she cursed because it was one of her guests who made her feel this way. She was treading on thin ice if she got involved with a paying customer, and even worse, with someone who was leaving in a few days. Maybe it was better this way. Rachel would be the first woman she would be with since Dale, and if things went badly in bed, she would not have to worry about accidentally running into her on the street or at Home Depot. God, how embarrassing would that be? Would they stand there and try to make small talk, each embarrassed by the whole thing, or would they each make a beeline for the next aisle to avoid each other?

Christina flirted with Shivley the entire way and didn't seem to mind or notice her one-word replies. Shivley found it amusing that a woman ten years her junior could be interested in a tired forty-two-year-old woman whose hands were calloused and whose skin had a permanent smell of horse and sweat and who wasn't even paying attention to her. When the barn was finally in sight, Shivley sighed in relief, tired of dodging innuendo after innuendo from her riding partner. She shook off her odd mood and turned in the saddle to face the group behind her. "Last one in the barn has to muck the stalls!"

Rachel and Sue were the first to pick up the challenge, and they kicked their mounts into action. As they flew by, Rachel's face was alive and flushed with excitement. Shivley's pulse quickly matched the speed of her horse. The other riders soon caught on, and once Shivley was comfortable that they would not suffer a spill, she raced to catch up with the leaders.

It wasn't long before Shivley passed Sue and caught up with Rachel, who was two lengths ahead of her. She nudged her horse and she rocketed ahead, quickly closing the gap. Midnight loved to run and would take off at the slightest signal. She was not even at full gallop when she came neck and neck with Bonanza.

Shivley glanced over at Rachel and her heart skipped a beat. Rachel's face was a study in concentration. Her eyes were barely visible under the brim of her hat and wisps of hair escaped out the back. To Shivley's trained eye, Rachel had the skill to be riding this fast, and she encouraged Midnight to run faster. The big horse quickly obeyed and they pulled away.

Rachel saw movement to her right but didn't take her eyes off the ground in front of her. She was unfamiliar with her horse and the terrain and didn't dare risk a fall by losing her concentration. After a moment, she didn't have to. A black quarter horse shot by her, its rider standing easily in the stirrups. She recognized the horse and then Shivley, and she spurred Bonanza to move ahead. The race was on.

They rode fast, exchanging the lead back and forth. Rachel was exhilarated and full of life as if she were riding away from her terrible childhood and her current troubles, her melancholy left behind with each step. She was free, with no worries, cares, or responsibilities. There were no cell phones ringing, cameras flashing, or people pressuring her to work magic. She let go of the reins with her right hand, pulled off her hat, and let out a loud "Yee haw!" She pulled ahead of Shivley and entered the corral first.

Rachel was laughing when Shivley rode up beside her, and Shivley was relieved to see her smiling again. Rachel's eyes were the color of the spring prairie and sparkled like the first star of the night. She was absolutely radiant when she smiled, and Shivley wanted to be the cause of that smile. "I knew you were a ringer when I first saw you."

Rachel batted her eyes and caught a lock of hair that cascaded across her eyes. "Why, whatever do you mean, Ms. McCoy?" She reverted to the soft Southern drawl she had used on Shivley once before. "I was just out for a little afternoon ride on my trusty steed." It was all Rachel could do to keep from bursting out laughing.

Shivley was caught up in the charade. She took off her hat and placed it over her heart. "I beg your pardon, Miss Stanton. I must have mistaken you for some other wildcat. What ever must I do to for your forgiveness?"

"Kiss me."

CHAPTER THIRTEEN

Shivley was speechless. She thought she had misunderstood what Rachel had said, but one look at her face convinced her otherwise. All charades were forgotten and Rachel was focused on her lips with an intensity that made Shivley's legs grow weak. If she weren't in the saddle, she might have collapsed in a heap. As it was, she had to press her legs together to stay upright. Midnight took that as a signal and moved forward, breaking the spell. "Whoa, girl." Shivley wasn't sure if her command was directed to her, her horse, or Rachel. She pulled back on the reins, her hat slipping from her hands and landing in the dirt.

Rachel had no idea what she was going to say until it came out of her mouth, and she was not sorry that it did. After this morning she had wanted nothing more than to pick up where they left off in the kitchen and see how far it would go. The cold shower suggested by Ann had done little to cool her libido, and being with Shivley all day stoked the fire.

"Now look what I've done." Rachel resumed her drawl. "It's my turn to apologize to you, Ms. McCoy, and ask what I can do for your forgiveness." She wanted Shivley, but she enjoyed toying with her more. It was not done in a mean-spirited way, but it was so refreshing to find someone who was honestly flabbergasted by her attentions. When Shivley didn't immediately answer, Rachel took pity on her. "You don't have to answer right now. Think about it and get back to me. Maybe tonight on the porch accompanied by an after-dinner drink?"

It was all Shivley could do to nod before the other women rode into the corral. They were excited from the race and were talking on top of each other. Christina was the first to mention that Ellen had come in last and to be sure to clean her horse's stall extra good. Everyone laughed at the frightened expression on Ellen's face.

"Don't worry, Ellen. I'll help." Shivley jumped in. The look of relief on Ellen's face was priceless. "Okay, everybody, walk your horses until they cool down, then take them into their stalls and give them a good brushing. I'll be along to see if you need any help."

Shivley spent time with each of the women as they tended to their horses, and before long the horses were brushed and fed and the tack put away. She made the mistake of stepping inside the stall where Christina was.

"Here, let me show you." Shivley took the brush from Christina's outstretched hand and briskly rubbed down the horse's sides. "Like this. Don't be afraid to rub hard. Dandy likes it that way."

Just then Christina stepped in close to her. "You can rub me like that anytime, Shivley. I know I'll like it as much as he does."

Christina was standing close enough that Shivley felt her warm breath on her neck. Instead of being provocative, it just gave her the shivers. She managed to slip past the eager woman and back out of the stall unscathed. She reminded herself she needed to be on high alert whenever Christina was around and to never be alone with her.

Shivley's last stop was at the stall adjacent to the one she just vacated. "Got everything you need?" she asked, standing on the threshold of the stall. Rachel spun around. The burning look on her face told Shivley that she had read more into her question than what was intended.

"Yeah, I'll be done in another minute or so."

Shivley had expected a reply more in line with the message that Rachel was giving her a few hours earlier, and she was surprisingly disappointed. As much as she wanted to kiss Rachel again, she was afraid. She was afraid of Rachel, and afraid of herself because she wanted much more than kisses. "He looks good."

"Excuse me?"

Shivley nodded toward the horse that gleamed under the brush of his rider. "Bonanza. I don't think I've ever see him so shiny and well cared for." She had been watching Rachel for several minutes brushing the horse. She was talking to him in soft, low tones that only the horse could hear, and Rachel had his undivided attention. A mask quickly fell over Rachel's eyes.

"Yeah, well, you know, horses, dogs, kids. All they need is a little love to survive," Rachel said and returned to brushing the buckskin.

Shivley had a hunch that there was more to Rachel than what people saw on the outside. Shivley was a pretty good judge of character, and her instinct told her that Rachel only allowed people to see exactly what she wanted them to see. Rachel's reserve was cracking, and Shivley wanted to know what was inside.

❖

Shivley walked through the great room after helping Ann clean up from dinner and counted six heads watching the big-screen television. Actually, it looked more like four of the six heads were dozing than watching the calm evacuation of the *Titanic*. Rachel was not in the room, nor had she given any indication of where she would be. Shivley gave it a passing thought but continued out the door.

The air was crisp as she walked across the yard toward the stables. A light was on and she made a mental note to remind Gail and Bart to turn it off when they were not inside. The sound of a soft voice drifted through the building and she quickened her pace.

Rachel was in Bonanza's stall brushing the buckskin and talking to him in hushed tones. Rachel didn't know she was there, and Shivley wanted to keep it that way for as long as possible. She watched as Rachel held the hard brush and stroked the horse across his back from the bottom of his mane to the top of his tail. Back and forth, back and forth, each stroke long and smooth, barely overlapping the one before. She was mesmerized by the calming strokes and the gentleness of Rachel's actions. A flash of Rachel's hands stroking her body in the same rhythm sent a chill down her spine. She suddenly felt very warm and her knees felt weak.

"I didn't think he'd mind a little more attention," Rachel said calmly, not turning around. She'd heard someone behind her, and when no words were spoken she knew it was Shivley. She had to concentrate to make sure her body didn't betray the way Shivley's presence affected her. If anything, she had never felt as sensual as she did right now knowing Shivley was watching her.

It took Shivley a moment to realize that Rachel was talking to her. She hadn't missed a stroke or even acknowledged that she knew Shivley was there. Shivley wondered how long

Rachel had known she was standing behind her. "What male wouldn't enjoy the skillful hands of a beautiful woman all over him?" Shivley almost gasped at her unfiltered reply. She was captured in Rachel's spell and couldn't get out. She detected a slight hesitation in Rachel's stroke before she turned to look at her. Her heart skipped a beat at the unmasked desire burning in Rachel's eyes.

"Does that apply to beautiful women ranchers?" Rachel licked her lips. She continued brushing Bonanza, accentuating each movement. Shivley had not moved, and Rachel wasn't sure she was even breathing. She slowly crossed the six feet that separated them and stopped just inches from Shivley's chest. She could see flecks of light reflecting in Shivley's dark eyes, which had not stopped staring at her lips.

Rachel stepped closer. "Do I frighten you?"

"Only when you look at me like you are right now." *And the way you did this morning, this afternoon, and yesterday, and the day before that.* Shivley racked her brain to remember the last time Dale had looked at her like that. Guilt trickled down her throat when she couldn't remember the last time she looked at Dale like that either.

Rachel cocked her head. "And how am I looking at you?"

Shivley swallowed the lump that had suddenly lodged in her throat. Her heart was pounding so loudly she could barely hear her own voice. She was treading on treacherous ground and her footing was shaky. "Like you want to kiss me."

"No, I don't want to kiss you." Rachel paused. "I want *you* to kiss *me*."

With one statement, Rachel turned Shivley's stomach upside down. Shivley wanted to kiss Rachel again but didn't think she was capable of taking the initiative. Her hands shook and she was afraid her legs would give out at any moment. It was hypocritical to want to be kissed but not be the kisser, but she didn't care. It took the responsibility out of her hands.

Rachel watched as it was apparent Shivley was struggling with what to do. She didn't think it had been a difficult request, especially after the kiss they shared that morning, but Shivley seemed to be hesitant.

"Rachel," Shivley began.

Rachel had had enough. She was tired, sore, and frustrated. "Shivley, what's really going on here?" With that comment, Shivley finally looked into her eyes. "No, don't look at me like you don't know what I'm talking about. You kissed me this morning. Quite passionately, I might add, and up until two seconds ago, you looked like you wanted to do it again. What's the deal? We're both consenting adults. I'm not attached and I don't think you are either, so why not have a little fun? And don't tell me it's because I'm a guest, because that's a smokescreen and you know it." Shivley didn't reply. Rachel wasn't used to women hesitating or turning her down, but she was not going to give up on Shivley. She knew she would be worth the wait. "Okay, I won't push it. At least not tonight."

CHAPTER FOURTEEN

S hivley was both relieved and disappointed as she
watched Rachel go back inside the house. She was a
coward. "Jesus, Shivley, a hot woman asks you to kiss her, and
you stand here quivering like a terrified virgin. Somebody slap
me before I stupid myself to death."

Shivley's arms felt like lead as she checked the other
horses before turning out the lights. She retraced her steps,
locked the front door of the house, and trudged up the stairs.
Several of the rooms she passed were dark, but light was
snaking out from beneath two others. She hesitated at Rachel's
door, listening for any sound that she was still awake. Shivley
had no idea what she would do if she was, but she listened
anyway. Not hearing anything to give her encouragement or
scare the hell out of her, she stepped across the hall to her own
room.

Rachel lay naked in bed in her darkened room waiting
for sleep to revive her tired body. She spent far too much
time behind a desk or on the campaign trail, and her body
was echoing that sentiment in stereo. She ached from one end

to the other, and definitely the places in between. She would never admit it to anyone, but she was grateful to get off her horse and sit in a soft, cushioned chair. The interesting thing was that she didn't feel any discomfort until the hours in the saddle were over. The joy of riding a horse again brought back memories she had long forgotten.

Rachel lay quietly on the bed when she heard the unmistakable sound of footsteps walking down the hall. She knew by process of elimination that it could be no other than Christina, and Rachel knew exactly where she was headed. The footsteps stopped and the sound of soft knocking quickly followed. Several seconds passed before she heard any noise indicating the occupant behind the closed door had heard the sound. The noise of the latch unlocking echoed in the hallway.

Rachel imagined Shivley opening the door to admit her caller, a warm, soft robe covering her clean, naked body. She listened but was unable to make out what the murmuring voices were saying, and it wasn't long before she heard the door close firmly. She waited for the sound of receding footsteps, and an unfamiliar pang of jealousy shot through her when she heard none. Unnerved by her wayward thoughts and the unusual feelings she was experiencing while on the ranch, Rachel didn't consider that she had not seen Shivley give any indication that she was interested in Christina. But then again, she had not been with Shivley every minute, and the young woman *was* hot, and if nothing else, persistent.

Rachel quickly shook the erotic thoughts from her head, and against her own will, listened for any sounds emanating from the room across the hall. Forty minutes later the only sound she heard was the natural creaking of the old house. Her body finally won the battle for sleep and she closed her eyes.

A collage of images danced through Rachel's dreams, all of them involving Shivley. In one scene Midnight was running at top speed, Shivley confidently in the saddle. In another it was the instant Shivley recognized her when she stepped off the plane. But most vivid was the image of Shivley in a blue pin-striped suit complete with silk stockings, her legs spread, lying on top of a desk.

The dream began with Rachel sitting across the desk from Shivley, an envelope bulging with papers on her lap. No words were spoken between them, but it was clear that Rachel had come to Shivley for her annual income tax preparation. Shivley stood and slowly walked around to the front of her desk. She lifted one leg and sat on the edge, settling mere inches from her. Rachel's gaze fell to the expanse of leg exposed by the provocative pose, and she ached with the need to touch the firm muscles encased in silk. When Shivley shifted, Rachel caught a glimpse of dark triangle through her sheer panties, and her throat closed.

Rachel watched the dream unfold as if she were an observer and not a participant. Shivley knew exactly what she was doing and moved again, opening her legs farther. Rachel's mouth fell open at the tantalizing view of Shivley's crotch, damp with arousal.

Rachel didn't remember exactly what happened, but the next thing she knew she was leaning over Shivley, one hand inside her blouse and the other up her skirt. The desk accessories were scattered on the floor and the telephone was ringing. Shivley's hands were in her hair pulling their kiss deeper and smothering the moans coming from deep within her. Her hand caressed the inside of Shivley's thighs, then traveled higher, the silk stockings providing an invitingly smooth path.

Shivley gasped and arched her back when she touched

her. The thin fabric of Shivley's panties were soaked with evidence of her arousal. Rachel dragged her mouth away from Shivley's hungry lips and quickly traveled down a creamy throat seeking breasts hidden beneath the silk blouse. Rachel couldn't get the buttons opened and instead pushed the blouse up to expose the waiting breasts. Shivley was not wearing a bra, and Rachel's tongue immediately traced a path around the base of Shivley's breast and continued the circular pattern until she finally rounded the peak.

Shivley's nipple was erect and hard in her mouth and Rachel lightly nibbled on it. Shivley moaned Rachel's name at the same time she grabbed a handful of her hair and pulled her lips closer. Rachel savored the taste of the breast in her mouth as her fingers snaked inside Shivley's panties. She was rewarded with a gush of liquid that coated the tips of her fingers. Her long, wet fingers explored every soft fold and warm valley at the same time her lips reclaimed Shivley's. Shivley broke the kiss and begged, "Go in me, please." Rachel wanted Shivley so badly she couldn't restrain herself from obeying the command.

Ever so slowly first one finger entered, then two, and were encased in warmth and wetness that she had never experienced. Rachel took her cue from Shivley, her fingers expertly matching the rhythm of Shivley's tongue darting in and out of her mouth. The big mahogany desk bucked in time with the two women fucking on the surface. Rachel could barely breathe and her hand was crushed when Shivley finally exploded in orgasm.

For the second time in almost as many days Rachel woke fully aroused and wired to explode. She didn't move, hoping to fall back asleep and return to the wonderful dream. After several minutes she knew it was fruitless, rolled onto her stomach, and looked at the clock. She had another fifteen minutes before her alarm was set to go off, and she debated between finishing the job her dream began and drowning her desire in the shower. She chose the former—or rather her body decided for her.

CHAPTER FIFTEEN

The only sounds at the breakfast table were the clinking of silverware and the intermittent sipping of coffee. The lack of conversation didn't surprise Shivley, considering it was five thirty in the morning, and she was pleased to see all of the women were present and accounted for. Several looked like they had stayed up past their bedtime, while others looked as though they hadn't slept at all. That was the category Shivley fell into, and she was not happy about it.

The knock on her door the night before was not totally unexpected, but the person doing the knocking was. She'd expected to see Rachel on the other side of the door and was surprised when it was not. It had taken her a moment to realize that she was disappointed that Christina was her caller and not the woman in the room across the hall.

Christina had been smooth in her approach the previous two days, using a combination of subtlety and frank gazes to get her point across. Last night when Shivley had not bitten, Christina stepped closer but immediately stopped when Shivley finally had to tell her point-blank thanks, but no thanks. Shivley had watched Christina silently walk away before closing her door and retreating to bed, where she stared at the ceiling most of the night.

Shivley observed Rachel over the top of her coffee cup, noting that she was not afraid to eat. Most women she knew who had a body like Rachel's would rather starve than work hard to keep the pounds away. Rachel put two more pieces of bacon on her plate and another pancake, and again Shivley realized that Rachel was the exception.

After breakfast Rachel and the other women saddled up their horses and spent an hour or so with Shivley giving them some basic instruction on rounding up stray cattle. Shivley watched for confirmation that the women understood what to do, how to do it, and what their horses had been trained to do. She warned them if they were not paying attention, their horse would cut left while they were still going right and the women would find themselves lying in the dirt wondering what happened. She lifted the rope from her saddle horn and grasped it tightly in her gloved hand. She demonstrated how to use the rope to get the attention of the stray and lead it in the right direction. She didn't attempt to teach them how to throw the lasso over the steer's head. That lesson was far too advanced for this group. Some of the women were disappointed, and she agreed to teach them once they returned to the ranch later that day. The women caught on quickly and soon they were on their way in search of strays.

Gail and Bart were along to keep an eye on the women, who split into three groups. Rachel and Jackie were with Shivley, and somehow Christina managed to make it an even four. Rachel was not surprised to see Christina practically glued to the hip with Shivley—after all, they had spent the night together. *Or had they?* She had observed the two women over breakfast and decided they didn't look like they had just spent a night filled with sex. At first Rachel thought Shivley simply didn't want anyone to know that she had slept with a guest, but there was something in her face and in the set of her jaw that indicated something very different was going on.

Rachel waited for her opportunity and spurred her horse forward. "I didn't have a chance to properly say good morning. Everybody seemed to be half asleep, you included."

Shivley had stiffened at the sound of approaching hoofbeats. She had thought that last night she had made it perfectly clear to Christina that she was not interested, but Christina had been dogging her all morning, and Shivley was growing weary of it. She relaxed as Rachel rode up beside her. "It's like that in the mornings. Most people aren't used to the exercise and clean air. Throw in a little excitement like roping and riding a two-thousand-pound animal, and they usually crash. Wait till we spend the night on the ground. Then see how everybody looks."

"So what's your excuse?" Shivley looked at Rachel with a question in her eyes. "You do this every day." Rachel waved her hand to indicate their surroundings. "Sit on a horse, ride around, and fix things. What's your excuse for looking like you were up all night?" To encourage Shivley's response, Rachel kept her tone light and teasing.

Shivley laughed. "I've never had my life described in quite those terms. Let's see, ride around and fix things." Shivley thought for a moment. "I guess some people could think that's all I do, and in some respects it's true."

"Well, were you?" Rachel was not going to let Shivley off the hook so easily. She wanted confirmation that her hunch was correct.

"Was I what?" Shivley forgot the original question when Rachel looked at her with that "don't bullshit me" expression on her face.

"Up all night?"

"Up all night? Me? No." Shivley shook her head. "I tossed and turned a few times, but other than that I slept like a rock." *And just lied like one, too.*

Rachel didn't know whether to believe Shivley or not. She knew it was Christina who'd knocked at Shivley's door, and she was positive she didn't hear footsteps leading away after the door closed.

She studied Shivley critically as if she were looking for the chink in her story, but Shivley held fast to it. "You look like you don't believe me."

Rachel was surprised Shivley called her on it. "It's really none of my business." She tried to sound convincing.

Shivley thought about her answer before she spoke. She glanced at the trail and then looked Rachel square in the eyes. "You're right, it is none of your business." She hesitated in order to give Rachel a chance to draw her own conclusions. "I didn't sleep with her."

Busted. Shivley had seen right through her, and Rachel didn't know whether to be pissed or embarrassed. She was good at not showing her hand too early, but it was obvious this time she'd failed. Her emotions overrode her logic at the thought of Shivley making love to Christina. "So you say," Rachel snapped in response, angry at herself.

Shivley was surprised at Rachel's snide comment. She removed her hat and ran her fingers through her damp hair before returning it to her head. "No, Ms. Stanton, I don't just say. It's a fact." Shivley wondered why it was important for her to convince Rachel that Christina had left without even entering her room.

"You just kiss them in the kitchen," Rachel shot back, still angry at herself.

"Wrong again. You kissed me." Shivley was surprised at her calmness. The image of them kissing shot into her brain.

This time it was Rachel who removed her hat and wiped her hand across her brow. "And I remember your tongue halfway down my throat." That really wasn't the case. As a matter of fact, it was her tongue that was doing most of the traveling. Her humor had returned and she wanted to see just how far Shivley would go to defend her honor.

"It was not!" Shivley exclaimed, louder than she intended.

"You're right, it wasn't. But I'd bet that if we hadn't been interrupted it would have been. And that would have been nice." Rachel licked her lips as if reliving their brief kiss. The flushed look on her riding companion's face told her she, too, remembered it clearly. Shivley started to say something, but Rachel held up her hand and cut her off. "I know, I know. You don't sleep with your guests. I get it." She winked and spurred her horse in the opposite direction.

❖

The two teams worked closely, and in between laughing at each other's antics and cursing the stubborn animals, managed to round up a dozen strays. Fortunately, everyone had paid attention to Shivley's briefing, and so far no one had found themselves looking at the underside of their horse. Three steers separated Shivley from Rachel, and they were calmly moving to join the others when one bolted and took off running. The remaining two took that as their signal and quickly scattered as well.

Shivley took off after the lead steer, uncoiling her rope with one hand while grasping the reins with the other. Her horse was practically at a full run, and she stood in the stirrups to use her legs to absorb the jolting movement. She swung the lasso around her head several times as she closed the gap between herself and the runaway. With a smooth toss perfected after hundreds of such tries, she looped the lasso, which fell over the steer's head. She quickly wrapped the remaining rope around the saddle horn and reined in her horse. The two animals came to a stop simultaneously amid cheers and applause.

Shivley turned around, and all ten women, along with Gail and Bart, were clapping and whistling. No matter how many times she chased one of the herd, it still thrilled her like it was the first time. She was breathing hard from the adrenaline rush. With her free hand she removed her hat and swung it in the air as if she had just snared the prize steer at the local rodeo.

Rachel watched the scene unfolding as if watching a movie. Shivley didn't hesitate when the steer made his break, and her sure, confident movements in the saddle were impressive. She knew exactly what to do, and at one point must have anticipated what the steer would do because she intercepted it in mid-stride. The rope soaring through the air was as light as a feather, and when it landed over the steer's head Rachel couldn't help but think of a basketball saying— "nothing but net."

The herd secure, the group stopped for lunch, quickly devouring the cold sandwiches, chips, and fruit Ann had packed for them that morning. Several lay down under the shade of a tree, stretched their tired limbs, and took a light nap while Gail and Bart kept an eye on the strays they had rounded up.

Shivley sat down on a fallen tree, and when Christina approached, gave her a look that clearly told her to find somewhere else to sit. Christina glared at her throughout the meal, which made Shivley feel slightly guilty, but not enough to do anything about it. It was Shivley's job to ensure all of her guests enjoyed themselves, and rebuffing one of them was not the way to do it. She would have to make up for it later, but right now she was simply too tired.

She thought back to her conversation with Rachel earlier

that morning. It was partially true. She had tossed and turned a few times last night, but that was before she gave up trying to sleep at all. Every time she closed her eyes she saw a blonde in boots, jeans, and a hat.

She leaned her back against the thick stump and must have dozed off because she came awake with a jerk at the sound of her name. Bart was calling her from across the stream, and Shivley quickly scanned the other women hoping no one had noticed she had fallen asleep. All the women were either napping or talking quietly to each other except Rachel, who was looking straight at her.

Rachel had been watching their sleeping host as she slowly inhaled and exhaled with each breath. Shivley's legs were stretched out in front of her, her hands lying casually in her lap, hat pulled low over her eyes. She looked like a real cowgirl, and a damn sexy one at that. Rachel smiled at that thought. *For crying out loud, she* is *a real cowgirl. Not a wannabe like the rest of us.* Rachel enjoyed the opportunity to study the lanky form uninterrupted and took her time imagining what the skin beneath the worn jeans and cotton shirt would feel like under her fingers. If it was anything like her dream the night before, she might die from the exquisite sensation. She sighed with disappointment when Shivley woke, ending observation.

Shivley was all business talking with Bart. Her stride across the creek had been purposeful, and her stance once she arrived was confident. Even though they were outside under the cloudless sky, Shivley had a presence about her that Rachel imagined would fill any room.

For the second time that day Shivley caught Rachel watching her. If it weren't for the rush of arousal, she would have felt uncomfortable at the attention. Several years ago a guest had stared at her the entire week, and after a few days,

Shivley felt as if she were being stalked. Thankfully, when the week was over, the woman disappeared from her life. But Rachel watching her was different. She stood a little taller and sat straighter in the saddle, all for Rachel's benefit. She was desired, a feeling that left her many years ago. She came back across the stream as the women began to stir.

"Okay, ladies, let's get these cattle back to the ranch and we'll call it a day."

Shivley had no preconceived ideas that it would be that easy, and she wasn't wrong. The cattle spotted a section of fence that was down, and the lead steer quickly headed in that direction. Shivley quickly rode to the front along the south side of the herd, Rachel parallel to her to the north. A wave of warmth mixed with déjà vu washed over her at the sight. She had imagined this scene in her head many times: working the ranch with the woman she loved by her side. The rider beside her had no face, but Shivley always knew it was not Dale.

Simultaneously they arrived at the lead steer and turned him and the herd around before they hit the open range. Shivley gave Gail and Bart instructions to take the women and the herd back to the corral while she stayed to repair the fence. When Shivley dismounted to repair the fence a shadow passed across her back.

"Need some help?"

The sun was behind Rachel, silhouetting her body, accentuating every womanly curve. The sight was almost more sensual than if she were standing there completely naked. A few strands of hair had escaped from her ribbon and blew in the gentle breeze. Shivley's throat tightened. "Sure. You should have some pliers in your saddle bags and some rope." Each woman had a small set of tools typically used every day on the ranch. Shivley found that it often came in handy, and today was no exception.

Rachel knew how to mend a fence and was quickly on the ground beside Shivley lifting posts and pulling wire without having to be told. Several times she was distracted by Shivley's bronzed muscles covered in a light sheen of sweat glistening in the sun, and more than once Shivley caught her looking.

Shivley was impressed. Not only could Rachel mend a fence, but she did it without complaining. She was strong, resourceful, and persistent. Shivley was accustomed to her guests working alongside her. It was a working dude ranch, after all. But working with Rachel beside her was very different. They worked well together. Rarely did Shivley have to tell her what to do, and when she did, Rachel understood immediately. This was what Shivley had envisioned when she dreamed of the ranch. But guilt was burning in her throat like bile. Guilt that she had never imagined Dale would be by her side and shame that now that she had met Rachel, Shivley wouldn't want her to be.

Rachel stood back to admire their handiwork. "Not bad for a couple of lesbians."

"Pretty damn good for a couple of girls," Shivley countered. She would return to this section tomorrow with the proper tools to secure their temporary handiwork.

"Touché. Right back at ya, Rancher McCoy." Rachel was proud of what they had done. She realized that it had been a long time since she had experienced a sense of accomplishment like this and even longer for something she could be proud of. Yes, she got people elected, but so what? What impact did she really make? Her job was difficult. Every one of her candidates had a skeleton in their closet, but she could hold the door closed with one hand and spin with the other with her eyes closed. Big deal.

She never stayed around to see the impact of what she had done. Those who dabbled in psychoanalysis would say that she was never held accountable for her actions. She didn't think that was entirely true. If she didn't produce, she was fired. But again, so what? A dozen more clients just like the one she left were waiting in line for her skills. Her job consisted of one campaign after another. Her personal life mirrored her professional one. She drifted from woman to woman, and after over twenty years as a lesbian, she had absolutely nothing to show for it. She didn't have any ex-girlfriend stories, no photographs on her coffee table of places she and a lover had visited on a romantic vacation. Her life was as transitory as her job. She was drifting, and until recently she thought nothing of it. As a matter of fact, it suited her. No demands, no commitments, and no disappointments. But lately she had an underlying need for something more permanent to wrap her arms around.

The last few days were filled with hard, physical work, pure and simple. At the end of the day there was a tangible result that she could be proud of. The difference between Washington and Arizona was much more than simple geography.

CHAPTER SIXTEEN

The cattle were in the holding pen and the horses set out to graze in the adjacent fenced pasture when Shivley and Rachel arrived back at the ranch. Several women were sprawled on the soft couches in the great room, and a few had made it up the stairs.

Shivley continued into the kitchen and headed straight for the refrigerator. The cool blast felt good on her sweaty skin. When she reached inside for some water, a voice behind her made her tingle.

"Got one for me, too?"

Shivley grabbed two bottles and turned around. "Certainly." She handed one to Rachel.

Rachel intentionally grasped both the bottle and Shivley's fingers and used her grip as leverage, pulling Shivley toward her. "The kitchen appears to be our place." Rachel fully intended to kiss the lips that had driven her crazy all day.

Shivley was not expecting the move, but smoothly sidestepped the approaching mouth, pulling her hand away and leaving Rachel hanging in midair.

"That wasn't very nice," Rachel replied once she had recovered from her awkward position. She unscrewed the cap and lifted the bottle to her lips.

Shivley lost whatever composure she had when Rachel tipped her head back, allowing the cold water to slide down her exposed throat. Rachel swallowed several times, and a trickle of water escaped and slid down the front of her neck. Shivley wet her lips, imagining her tongue catching the droplet that was disappearing into the V of Rachel's shirt. She was envious of its path and watched Rachel's chest as if she could see it through the soft material.

Rachel released the bottle from her lips, almost choking as she swallowed the remaining water. The expression on Shivley's face was a mixture of lust and apprehension, with lust winning out as the dominant feature. The familiar surge of arousal leaped at her, and Rachel was instantly wet simply from Shivley looking at her. Her nipples tightened under Shivley's intent gaze.

Shivley's body responded to the tension that filled the air. Her breath came in short bursts and her knees grew weak. Her vision excluded everything around her except for the rise and fall of Rachel's breasts. She didn't know who was mimicking whom, but Rachel's chest was moving in time with hers. Warm liquid sped through her veins and settled in the crotch of her Levi's. She grasped the edge of the counter with one hand to steady herself while the other still held the bottle of water. Her grip was so tight the plastic started to crack in protest.

"Jesus Christ, would you two take it upstairs?"

Shivley reacted first. She didn't know whether to laugh or cry. To be publicly rebuked was humiliating, and she felt like she'd just been caught making out under the bleachers with the head cheerleader.

"For God's sake, you're two consenting adults. Stop

fighting it and just do it. I'm tired of you using my kitchen as an erogenous zone."

"Ann," Shivley began. She wasn't doing anything, so why should she feel guilty?

"What? Oh come on, Shivley. This is the second time I've walked in on you two, and both times if I would have come in five minutes later, you'd have been on the floor, and you know it."

"That's not the point. Rachel is—"

"Jesus, would you stop with the guest thing?" Rachel interrupted Shivley before she could continue. "You're right. I am the guest, and the guest is always right. So stop treating me like one." Rachel shook her head at the absurdity of her statement. Shivley and Ann simultaneously turned their attention to Rachel. "For crying out loud, stop acting like you're going to offend me. I'm capable of making my own decisions." She directed her comments to Shivley. "I *want* to kiss you. As a matter of fact, I want to do more than kiss you, and at the risk of offending *your* sensibilities, a good fuck is exactly what *I* need."

All three women burst out laughing at the same time, releasing the tension in the room. Shivley finally had to sit down before she fell down, she was laughing so hard. Rachel and Ann joined her around the table, and they started laughing again. Shivley finally pulled herself together.

"Ann, do you have anything else to say?" Shivley held up her hands. "No, don't answer that. I'm certain that you do."

"You still don't think you hired me for my cooking, do you? You needed me then and you really need me now." Ann cast Shivley a look that said, *And you know what I'm talking about.*

Shivley relied on Ann's keen insight and often conferred with her on personal and ranch matters. She shrugged.

"Obviously." She cast a quick glance at Rachel, *a good fuck is exactly what I need* echoing in her brain.

Rachel smiled. "You hired her."

"Whatever was I thinking?" Shivley dropped her head into her hands.

Rachel noted that the twinkle had returned to Shivley's eyes. "We all make mistakes. The question should be, why is she still here?"

Shivley was enjoying turning the tables on her friend. "Because she makes a killer bologna sandwich."

"That's exactly why you keep me around. Now, it's time for me to start dinner. You two take your insightful conversation somewhere else, or I'll put you to work." Ann had a dish towel in her hand and snapped it at Shivley. She shook her head in disbelief. "You can birth a calf and fix a tractor, but you can't boil water worth a damn. Now scoot."

Shivley knew when it was time to leave Ann's kitchen, and this was it. She got out of the chair expecting Rachel to follow. "Don't tell me you do know how to boil water?"

Rachel sat back with a smug look on her face. "Uh-huh. And not only do I know how to boil water, but I can even toast bread." She flashed Shivley a playfully superior look.

"Okay, okay, I know when I'm beat, again, as a matter of fact. I'll just mosey out to the barn and fix something. At least there I'm pretty good at what I do." She kissed Ann on the cheek on her way out.

The banging of pots and pans was uncharacteristically soothing for Rachel. She was not domestic in the slightest, and the only thing in the cookware in her house was dust. "Would you like some help?"

Ann looked over her shoulder. "Would you know what to do if I said yes?"

"Probably not, but I can follow directions."

Ann laughed and waved her knife at Rachel. "Thanks, but I think I can handle it. Just go and enjoy yourself. Why don't you take a soak in the Jacuzzi before dinner?"

Rachel was tempted but knew better. "If I did that now I'd never get out. But thanks for the suggestion. I think I'll just wander around a bit. See you at dinner."

CHAPTER SEVENTEEN

Shivley was bent over a John Deere tractor, her head under the hood, her ass in perfect position for Rachel to stare at as she leaned against the doorjamb. She crossed her arms over her chest and settled in to enjoy the view. The brim of her hat deflected the afternoon sun, but a bead of sweat snaked down her back and into the waist of her jeans. Rachel had watched Shivley for most of the day, and the more she did, the more intrigued she was about the owner of this wonderful ranch.

She glanced around the barn and noted it was as well kept as the stables. Various hand tools hung on hooks attached to Peg-Board behind the workbench. Several hooks were vacant, their occupants scattered on the ground at Shivley's booted feet. Shivley's hand searched blindly along the fender, missing a wrench several times. "A little more to your right."

Shivley jerked up, hitting her head on the hood of the tractor. "Ouch, shit." She lifted her hand and rubbed her head, smearing grease on her cheek. Rachel stepped forward and offered her a shop rag. "Thanks."

"Sorry. I didn't mean to startle you. It looked like you needed some help. What are you working on?"

The sight of Rachel standing in her barn like she belonged there made it difficult for Shivley to follow the chain of Rachel's conversation. "The engine's got a slight ticking when she first starts up."

"I'd offer to help, but I already tried that with Ann, and she just about threw me out." Rachel chuckled at the memory.

Shivley wiped her hands. "She's very protective of her domain. She's not nearly as mean as she pretends to be."

"She seems to be pretty protective of you."

"We've been friends a long time. Sometimes I'm not sure if she's my friend or trying to be my mother." Shivley recalled many times where it was the latter, and she inwardly thanked her for it.

A stab of long-forgotten pain centered in Rachel's belly. Her reaction to Shivley's comment startled her. As a little girl and even into her young adulthood, Rachel would flinch at any mention of the friends and family she never had. She often made up stories in her head to ease the loneliness she experienced whether she was alone or in the middle of a crowded room. "You're lucky." Rachel barely got the words out.

"Excuse me?"

Rachel didn't realize she had spoken out loud, and by the expression on Shivley's face she wasn't going to be able to fake her way out of it. "I said that you're lucky to have a friend like that."

There was something behind Rachel's simple comment that Shivley wanted to explore, but a smelly barn, up to her elbows in engine grease, was probably not the most conducive scenario for deep conversation. "I am." Shivley wanted to say more but was tongue-tied at the prospect of an intimate conversation with Rachel. She took the safe way out. "Something tells me you know the difference between a crescent wrench and a box head."

Rachel knew Shivley had seen her reaction, and she inwardly thanked her for not pressing the issue. "Yes, I do. In fact I'm pretty familiar with tools, and better yet, know how to use them." Rachel was very self-sufficient with repairing things, and at one home had helped rebuild a 1965 Mustang. But it was her last comment that opened Shivley's eyes wide, and she knew she had struck her mark.

"Uh, okay, uh, I'd like to uh, get this fixed by the time Ann hollers at us for dinner." Shivley knew she was stammering all over herself, the image of Rachel and tools bouncing through her brain.

Rachel removed her hat and tossed it on the workbench. "Great, what do you need?"

❖

Both women stood with their hands on their hips listening to the tractor purring quietly. For the second time that afternoon Shivley was amazed at how well they had worked together. Rachel seemed to know exactly what she needed when, and she often felt the cool, hard tool in her hand before she asked for it. Their conversation was strictly mechanical as Rachel asked and Shivley answered questions about the engine and its parts.

"It sounds great."

"That's the way she's supposed to sound. Thanks for your help. Without you I probably would have been out here after dinner, too."

"Flattery will get you anywhere, and I appreciate it, but all I did was hand you the tools."

"Don't sell yourself short, Rachel." Shivley put the tools back on their respective pegs. "You knew exactly what I was doing, sometimes even before I did. I've got you figured out."

"Do tell," Rachel said leaning on the tractor.

"You're really a mechanic for a NASCAR driver and are masquerading as a political strategist." Shivley gave Rachel her best cloak-and-dagger look.

Rachel smiled. "Busted."

Shivley broke out in laughter. "If you wanted to lay low I would have thought you'd have picked something a little less controversial for your cover."

Rachel joined in Shivley's amusement. "Well, I'm not known for my conservatism."

"What are you known for?" Shivley asked, wiping the remaining grease off her hands.

"A little of this and a little of that," Rachel answered evasively.

Shivley frowned. She knew she had no reason to be, but she was hurt by the flippant answer. Rachel didn't owe her any explanation, and Shivley certainly wasn't one to throw the first stone.

Over the years Rachel had mastered the art of vagueness to the point of perfection, keeping people from delving deeper into her life. She recognized that Shivley was hurt by the answer, and for the first time, it bothered her. Rachel decided to change that.

"Actually, I spent a summer restoring an old car, everything from new windshield wipers to repairing the transmission." The look of surprise and admiration on Shivley's face gave her the confidence to continue. "I found that not only did I like it, I realized that I had a knack for anything mechanical. I'm probably the only person in my building that repairs their leaky faucet without calling 1-800-plumber."

"Well, aren't you something? First you whip me in a

horse race, you know how to mend a fence, and now you're a seasoned mechanic. What are you going to be tomorrow, a rocket scientist?" Shivley was not just being polite, she really wanted to know.

Rachel approached Shivley. "I guess you'll just have to wait and find out. A girl's gotta keep something mysterious up her sleeve, don't you think?" She stopped just inches in front of Shivley.

Shivley's body reacted to the nearness of Rachel in the way she had quickly come to recognize in the past few days. Her mouth was suddenly dry, and swallowing became difficult. "I suppose," she responded weakly.

Rachel stepped closer and ran her fingers up the outside of Shivley's forearm. "Do you want to know what I have up my sleeve, Rancher McCoy?"

"You don't have any sleeves, Ms. Stanton." Rachel had removed her shirt earlier so as not to get it soiled from grease and was standing before her in a sleeveless T-shirt. Shivley was amazed that she was able to form a coherent thought, let alone have it cleverly and clearly come out of her mouth.

"You're much too literal, Rancher McCoy. Must be the CPA in you." Rachel paused. "Let me rephrase the question. Since I don't have sleeves, do you want to know what I have hiding inside my shirt?"

Shivley's eyes dropped to Rachel's chest. "Is it a surprise?" *God, what a stupid thing to say.*

Rachel turned her caress of Shivley's arm from the outside to the soft, sensitive inside of her arm from elbow to wrist. "Do you like surprises?" Her nipples hardened under Shivley's focused gaze.

"Yes." It came out more like a croak than a word.

"Are you a patient woman?" Rachel asked.

"No," Shivley replied emphatically. She was overcome

with desire and closed the distance between them. Rachel's lips were as soft and warm as she remembered. Rachel's arms came around her neck, and Shivley encircled her waist. Rachel pushed her pelvis into Shivley's thigh together with a moan of desire, and Shivley smothered it with her kiss.

Shivley slipped her thigh higher into Rachel's crotch, sliding her hands under her damp T-shirt. She was instantly rewarded with warm, soft flesh that came alive under her fingertips. Rachel's tongue slipped into her mouth and Shivley countered by sliding her hands up and down Rachel's back. As Rachel devoured her mouth, Shivley explored taut stomach muscles, her hands quivering as she softly brushed the underside of full breasts, and when her thumbs lightly brushed tight nipples, Rachel bit her tongue.

Shivley spun them both around, reversing their positions, pinning Rachel to the hard workbench. She dragged her mouth away, breathing heavily, and began kissing Rachel's neck. Rachel inhaled sharply when Shivley ran her tongue down the side of her neck. Shivley placed passionate kisses along Rachel's jawline and returned to her waiting lips. Rachel's breasts fit perfectly in her hands.

Rachel was smoldering and Shivley was the match. Shivley's exploring hands were making her crazy, her nipples rock hard in Shivley's palms. She couldn't get enough of Shivley's mouth and wanted her lips all over her body. A blast of air hit her exposed stomach and she shivered. Shivley started to pull away. "No, don't stop."

Shivley had no intention of stopping and shifted her attention to the hot burning skin under her hands. She raised Rachel's shirt and simultaneously lifted her onto the bench. Rachel's breasts were in perfect alignment with her seeking mouth, and Rachel met her halfway.

CHAPTER EIGHTEEN

Shivley nibbled greedily on the nipple in her mouth. She missed the feeling of a woman in her arms responding to her caresses, and she quickly forgot about everything except the taste of Rachel. She lifted Rachel's shirt over her head and tossed it to the side, providing her clear access to Rachel's other breast.

"Oh God," Rachel called out when Shivley's tongue flicked over the sensitive surface. It was all she could do to remain upright as Shivley feasted on her warm flesh, traveling back and forth, and paying equal attention to both breasts.

Shivley's senses were filled with the taste, touch, and smell of Rachel, and she was desperate for her fill. She traced a path up Rachel's long neck and captured lips that immediately opened under hers. Her hands circled behind Rachel's back and dropped to her waistband. Rachel's tongue snaked in and out of her mouth and her passion skyrocketed. Rachel pulled Shivley's shirt, freeing it from her pants, and Rachel's nails quickly followed the path of exposed flesh. Shivleye inhaled sharply as Rachel's fingernails scratched her back. She shifted slightly, and her right hand drifted between Rachel's legs.

Rachel couldn't remember ever wanting a woman's mouth on her as much as she wanted Shivley's. Her hands shook as she grasped the soft curls and pulled the lowering head to her. Wet lips met flesh, and an electric bolt of pleasure shot directly to her crotch. After a few moments her hands dropped behind her onto the hard surface, and she unconsciously lifted her hips and arched her back.

Rachel broke away from the kiss at Shivley's first touch. Through the thick inseam of her jeans, she felt the slow, sensuous stroking and her body responded immediately. Her panties were wet and it would not be long before they soaked through onto Shivley's fingers. Just thinking about that sent another wave from her body. "God yes, Shivley, touch me."

The sound of Rachel's voice broke through the haze of passion, and Shivley stopped her wandering mouth and hands. She breathed heavily into Rachel's neck as she fought to regain control of her body and her mind. She was suddenly aware that Rachel was half dressed and that anyone could walk in on them at any moment, which brought her to her full senses.

Rachel's world stopped spinning and her mind began to focus. She had never been so aroused by so little foreplay. She was stunned to realize that she was on the edge of orgasm and would have crossed over in another minute or two if Shivley hadn't stopped. Rachel's body was wired tightly, but she was surprisingly relieved at the same time. She had had sex in stranger places, but she wanted the first time with Shivley to be something other than a fast fuck on a workbench.

Rachel spoke first. "Jesus, please don't tell me you're sorry again."

Shivley swallowed twice to clear her throat. She sighed deeply before answering. "No, I'm not, but I wish this was happening somewhere a little more private." Shivley stepped away, forcing herself to not look at the naked breasts in front of her. She handed Rachel her shirt and turned around to pull herself together.

Rachel's hands shook as she turned her shirt right side out and pulled it over her head. "What did you say?" Her blood was pounding in her ears so loudly she wasn't certain she'd heard Shivley's response correctly.

The rustling behind her ceased and Shivley cautiously turned around. It would not do her any good to be tempted with Rachel's body again, and she was relieved to see Rachel fully clothed. Rachel's hair was disheveled from Shivley's hands and her lips were swollen from their kisses. "I can't believe we were doing this out here where anyone could have walked in on us. I'm sorry. It could have been very awkward for you."

"But?" Rachel asked, picking up on her hesitation.

"But nothing. We're attracted to each other, and as you said earlier, two consenting adults." Shivley kicked at the straw on the floor of the barn.

"And?" Rachel didn't want any confusion or morning-after regrets.

"And I want to do it again." Shivley pierced Rachel with eyes that clearly spoke her intent. "But not here." She indicated their rough surroundings.

Rachel was elated at the confession. There was no doubt that Shivley wanted her, and she knew neither one of them would be disappointed. "Your place or mine?"

Shivley didn't know whether to laugh or cry. She was trying to move on with her life, and the first woman she was attracted to dropped a *line* on her. *Your place or mine? Jesus Christ.* She was saved from responding when Ann rang the dinner bell. Shivley had picked up the cast-iron bell in an antique shop with pure ornamental intent, but once the bell was hung, Ann immediately began using it, stating she was tired of hollering when meals were ready. The sound could be heard all over the grounds.

Shivley jumped at the escape the distraction provided. "We should be going in. Ann hates it when we're late and dinner gets cold." Shivley took a few steps toward the barn door, hoping Rachel would follow.

Rachel was puzzled at Shivley's change of manner. One minute she was crawling all over her and admitting she wanted more, and the next she was distant, almost grateful for the interruption. Rachel was pissed. *I don't have time for this shit.* She hated it when a woman either didn't know what she wanted or was afraid to go after it. She had not misread Shivley. When the ranch owner kissed her, she knew exactly what she wanted.

CHAPTER NINETEEN

Shivley walked across the yard and could feel Rachel's eyes boring into her back with every step. Her heart was pounding, her mouth was dry, and her head was spinning. Her boots made soft crunching noises over the small rocks, and she felt like she was walking to the gallows. Walking away from Rachel was one of the hardest things she'd ever done, and the farther away she got from her, the colder reality became. She couldn't simply have sex with Rachel. She would be leaving in a few days, and then what? Shivley was no prude, but the thought of a quickie, actually more of a short-term affair, didn't seem right. Although sleeping with Rachel seemed to be uncomplicated on the surface, it was really more than it appeared.

Shivley often talked to herself when she was struggling with a difficult situation. It made her think more clearly, and she definitely needed a clear head. "Jesus, Shivley, get a grip. You're forty-two years old, not some teenager who can't keep her pants zipped. You're a respectable woman with a successful business. Fucking in the barn is simply not your style. You deserve better than that." Shivley stepped onto the porch, hesitating before she reached for the doorknob. *And Rachel does, too. And she's leaving soon.* The mere thought of Rachel's imminent departure made Shivley anxious. She wanted her to stay longer. She wanted to get to know her better, to learn everything about her. She wanted to make love to her without the threat of time hanging over them. The ticking of the clock in her head had only gotten louder.

❖

Shivley sat in her usual spot at the head of the large dining room table and toyed with her food. She wasn't hungry, and going by the amount of food left on Rachel's plate, neither was she. Rachel had not spoken to her when she returned to the house and had barely acknowledged any of the other women sitting around the table. They didn't seem to notice Shivley and Rachel were not active contributors to the chatter.

Cindy sat to her left, followed by Joyce, Sue, and Christina. Jane, Debra, Jackie, Becky, and Ellen were to her right, with Rachel at the opposite end of the table. The women had hearty appetites after several days of hard work and they helped themselves to seconds of just about everything Ann served. Shivley observed each woman. Their physical attributes were obviously different, but the most compelling difference was their personalities.

Ellen laughed, pulling Shivley's attention back to the table. Cindy, Joyce, and Jane had similar personalities, while Debra, Jackie, and Sue had the best senses of humor. Becky was an introvert, Christina was moody, and Ellen the peacemaker. Shivley looked at each woman and went through a mental checklist of comparisons to Dale.

There were absolutely no similarities between Rachel and Dale other than the fact that they were both women. And that they had both kissed her, Shivley thought wryly. She focused on that and immediately realized that she shouldn't have. Yes, they had both kissed her, but that was where the similarity ended. One had done it out of habit, the other out of desire and need.

Ann poured coffee, giving Shivley a break from her thoughts, but not for long. As soon as their cups were filled, it dawned on Shivley that maybe this was why she refused to get involved with one of her guests. And in the past few years, she'd had plenty of opportunity. She thought back to the other women who had sat around this table, and Shivley suddenly realized that she had compared all of them to Dale. That was something she consciously found herself doing in the first few months after Dale died, but not lately. Of course they had all paled in comparison to Dale in one way or another, but this time Dale was the one who was less than perfect.

Shivley fought against the sting of guilt that threatened to become a full-fledged case of shame. Dale had died, left everything to her, and Shivley had continued on with her life. And moving on included someone to share it with. It didn't include Dale, but it never would have in the first place. Would she continue to compare every woman to Dale? Was she using propriety as a shield so she wouldn't have to deal with the fact that she was happier without Dale than she was with her?

Shivley looked at Rachel, and she was afraid. Would she see Dale's face if they made love? Would she compare lovemaking techniques? A sense of humiliation shot through Shivley as if it had actually happened. She couldn't do that to Rachel. Jesus, she couldn't do that to anyone. She looked around the table again. She loved having her house filled with the laughter of women who loved each other. She wanted Rachel here at the table with her every night. She wanted to make love under the stars with Rachel, and not as some guest that she would never see again.

Rachel watched the emotions play across Shivley's face like clouds passing in the sky. Shivley would not make a good politician; her emotions were too transparent. Rachel was crossing off the range of emotions going through her as well. There was lust, confusion, anger, then desire, back to anger, the pattern repeating. She was hot and cold and watched as Shivley was on and off as well. Thank God she only wanted to fuck, not get married. She was not in the practice of psychoanalyzing her feelings. Getting into her bedmate's head was not what she was interested in. She was not into fixing her temporary partner's "issues." God, she had enough issues of her own. The only issue she did want to fix was the need to release months of pent-up sexual energy.

❖

Shivley walked across the yard and stopped at the corral. She put her foot up on the bottom rail and rested her forearms on the warm wood. She knew she had been an ass to Rachel during dinner. She knew she needed to do something, she just didn't know what. Something had to change and it had to change soon.

"A quarter for your thoughts."

"Why so much?"

"Haven't you been keeping up with the cost of inflation? A penny doesn't buy what it used to, you know."

Shivley laughed, easing some of the tension in the air. Rachel moved into her peripheral vision and she, too, rested her arms on the top rail. They both looked at the stars.

"Where did you grow up?" Shivley asked quietly.

"Everywhere."

"Are you always so evasive?" Shivley hoped her question didn't sound as accusatory as it could have.

Rachel opened her mouth to snap a reply but instead said, "Only when people get too close."

Shivley took a sip of her coffee. "Asking where you grew up is getting too close?"

Rachel hesitated and made a pivotal decision. "When you're the property of the state of Montana it is." Rachel read the question in Shivley's eyes. "I lived in nine foster homes and went to eight schools by the time I was fifteen." Rachel was tired just saying it.

"I'm sorry."

"For what? You don't know me." Rachel's defense mechanisms kicked into high gear.

"Does anyone?" Shivley asked quietly.

"What the fuck does that mean?" Rachel was angry. *How dare she act like she knows anything about my life?*

Shivley didn't answer. The tension in the air was thick. "Why are you here, Rachel?"

"Rest, relaxation, fresh air, hard work. Everything your glossy brochure described." Rachel crossed her arms across her chest, her right side against the rail. She saw Shivley smile.

"I'm glad my ad works, but in your case, I think that's bullshit."

Rachel started to say something scathing, but something held her back.

Shivley repeated her question. "Why are you here, Rachel?"

Rachel's insides felt as if a rusty gate was trying to swing open. "I spent a few years on a ranch when I was a teenager. It was probably the best foster home I had the entire twelve years I was in the system. When I first arrived at the Stewarts' I was a smart-ass, hard-core thirteen-year-old. No one could tell me anything. I mean, my shit did not stink. And after a few days of mucking stalls and shoveling shit, I knew I was right.

In comparison to horse shit and cow dung, mine didn't stink. It was definitely roses.

"But I loved it there. It was like I was a totally different person. I couldn't wait to get up every day. Mr. Stewart had to practically drag me into the house in the evening to do my homework. Being there taught me so much. Not just how to ride a horse or use a rope but how to respect nature. How to live off the land. How it is our responsibility to give back. It gave me a sense of peace I haven't been able to find again." Rachel could see the ranch and her three years there as clearly as if it were yesterday.

"I feel out of sorts lately. Lost and discontent. What used to make me happy doesn't anymore." Rachel had never uttered those words to another person.

"What did?" Shivley asked cautiously.

"Power, fame, beating the other guy. Women." Rachel rattled off the main drivers of her life for the past few years.

"What did you do when you got out of the system?" Shivley asked, bringing the conversation back to Rachel's childhood.

"Fell through the cracks for a few years. One day you're a child, not capable of taking care of yourself, at least in the eyes of the state, and the next day you're an adult. A lot of kids are out on the street with nothing the day they turn eighteen. No home, no family, nothing. I was lucky. I had a decent job and had saved some money. I got a dumpy apartment, tried to keep my nose clean, and worked my way through college." Rachel summarized six years of her life in just a few sentences.

The crickets chirped in the distance and one of the horses in the barn whinnied, breaking the otherwise silent night. "How did you get into politics?"

Rachel couldn't believe how much she was opening up to Shivley. She had never told anyone half of what she was telling her. Being here on the ranch had done that to her. "College. I have a degree in political science, but I always knew I wanted to be behind the scenes. I got a break with a local politician running for reelection, and fifteen years later here I am, standing under the stars with a beautiful woman."

Shivley finally turned and looked at Rachel. "Are you finding what you're looking for?"

"I'm not sure I'd know it if I saw it. It could be standing right in front of me and I can honestly say I might not recognize it." Rachel had had enough baring of her soul for tonight and turned the conversation around to focus on Shivley. "Why are you here?" She knew the basic story from their conversation the other night, but she suspected there was more to it than that.

Shivley told Rachel about Dale, her illness, how she bought the ranch and developed it to what it was today. She never once looked at Rachel, but she could feel her soft eyes watching her.

"Do you miss her?"

The question was not what Shivley expected Rachel to say. Usually she got a variant of "I'm sorry for your loss," but no one had ever asked if she missed her. "No." The simple word shocked her. She hadn't even thought about her answer and certainly hadn't thought it would be no. Rachel didn't say anything.

"I mean not here. This ranch was my dream, not Dale's. She was never here, literally or figuratively. I miss being with someone. Not just the sex." Shivley peeked at Rachel, who had a very skeptical look on her face. "Okay, I miss the sex, but I also miss the idea of having someone in my life."

"How so?" Rachel asked. She had never missed anyone except her mother, and then only in the beginning.

"Just knowing there is someone there. Even if they are

hundreds of miles away, they're still with you." She lifted her chin. The night was clear and thousands of stars twinkled in the black sky. "You could be in Paris, and me right here, and we'd see the same stars."

The longing in Shivley's voice tugged at Rachel. She had never felt this way about another person and wondered if that was good or bad. "I wouldn't know."

Shivley turned and looked at Rachel standing beside her. It was comfortable being with Rachel this way, the moonlight illuminating her face in soft shadows.

"I never had a best friend or anyone that cared for me like that." Reality was as cold as it sounded.

"What about your parents?"

"My father was MIA from the get-go, and my mother, well, all I know about her is that she left me with a neighbor, told me she'd come right back, and never did. Needless to say, trust is not something I'm real familiar with."

Shivley wanted to hug Rachel but knew she would be rebuffed if she tried. Rachel wouldn't want her sympathy. "What about a lover?"

Rachel smirked. "Too many to count, none that ever did." She knew Shivley would not be judgmental of her past. Another long pause filled the night. "What about your family?" Rachel had never asked that question of anyone that she could remember. She wanted to know the answer now.

"My father is a first-class asshole, and for some reason, my mother has put up with him for forty-six years. Dad rules the house, is opinionated and a constant embarrassment. I stopped inviting friends over when I was fifteen."

"Any siblings?"

"One brother in Pittsburgh. Frank is a chip off the old block." Shivley had two nephews she had never seen, preferring to not subject herself to Frank's bigoted diatribes.

"How did they react when they found out you were a lesbian?" Rachel had been lucky to be with an understanding foster family when she came out. If they hadn't been, she could only imagine what her life would have been like.

Shivley turned around, her back to the corral fence. She put her hands in the front pockets of her jeans. "Dad hit me, Mom cried, and my brother got a hard-on. I was seventeen. Like you, I worked my way through college, had a girlfriend here and there, got my CPA, worked for a few jerks, started my own firm, met Dale, she died, and that just about brings you up to date."

"How long were you two together?" It was odd that Rachel was asking questions about an ex-lover. Whenever she had before it was only to inquire about sexually transmitted diseases.

"Four years. We dated for one and lived together for three."

"Were you happy?"

It took several moments for Shivley to answer the question. Images of her and Dale sharing laughter, love, and tears flashed in her mind. "I thought I was."

"What changed your mind?" Rachel's curiosity increased.

Shivley looked at her house across the yard. She'd designed the structure herself, along with the barn and the shed. She had set almost every fence post, hammered every nail, and selected every head of stock. It was more than she could imagine. "This. This is what changed my life. This is where I want to be for the rest of my life."

Rachel looked around as well and took a deep breath. "I'm with you."

Shivley wished Rachel meant it exactly the way she said it. She wanted Rachel by her side, to share the ranch with her. She wanted to spend peaceful nights like this with her and wake up next to her every morning. She reached out and touched Rachel's arm. "I'm sorry…for this afternoon… tonight." Shivley wasn't sure what to say. Rachel's soft smile warmed her.

"It's okay. Our demons never surface at an appropriate time. Good night."

Shivley watched Rachel walk toward the house. She wanted her and had no idea what to do about it. Rachel was leaving in five days.

CHAPTER TWENTY

The women had been riding for two hours when Shivley stopped for their first break. It was their fifth day at the ranch and they were headed to the north pasture to bring in the herd for shots and tagging. Rachel was surprisingly well rested. After her confession the night before, she was expecting to toss and turn all night but instead slept the best she had in months.

Shivley, on the other hand, looked terrible. Dark circles were pronounced under her eyes and she kept shooting glances at Rachel that she didn't understand. They had not had any opportunity to say anything other than a polite good morning to each other.

As Rachel rode that morning she wondered if she would ever need someone the way Shivley had described last night. She never let herself get that close to anyone. It simply hurt too much. She didn't remember much about her mother other than the pain she felt when she left. Even at the age of five, Rachel knew she would never see her mother again. The pain was almost as fresh as it was that cloudy day.

One lover she had let get too close thought she could change her. Rachel had made it very clear that she was not looking for a relationship and when she ended it, the woman flew into a rage. She said many things, most of them very ugly, and said that Rachel needed to "see someone," as she phrased it, to get help for her commitment phobia. Rachel didn't need a shrink to tell her that her mother's abandonment and her unstable childhood were the cause. Anything she ever cared about was ripped from her. Rachel simply chose not to repeat the cycle. For her entire childhood she had no choice in anything concerning her life, but the one thing she could control was her feelings. She kept them exactly where she wanted them to be. It was as simple as that.

There were a few groans as the women dismounted and led their horses to the watering trough. The troughs were scattered across the ranch, providing fresh water for the horses and cattle as they roamed freely.

"There's nothing in here," Joyce said, confused.

"Shit." Shivley dismounted and walked over to the trough. It was fed from a natural stream with a float that kept it from overflowing, but right now it was bone dry. From what she could see, the float arm was corroded and was stuck in the closed position.

"Hmm. Even I don't think it's supposed to look like that." Rachel had walked up behind Shivley without her noticing.

"Right again, Miss *I am full of surprises and can fix anything*," Shivley teased. She had enjoyed her conversation with Rachel last night and her spirits were high. "What do you suggest we do?"

Rachel grinned at the teasing moniker. "Joyce, do you have any of that Coke left?" she asked, not directly answering Shivley's question. Joyce handed her the can, and Rachel slowly poured the contents over the corroded area. Bubbles erupted, accompanied by a slight hissing sound as the beverage ate away at the offending material. In just a few moments the float lifted and water started pouring into the trough.

"I'll be damned." Shivley shook her head. Rachel continued to amaze her.

Rachel crushed the can under her boot and picked it up. "Anything else, boss?" She glowed at the surprised look on Shivley's face. It thrilled her to keep Shivley off her stride. Rachel was rarely challenged by a woman, but being here on Shivley's ranch was nirvana. "Better watch out, boss. I'm not your average, everyday spin doctor, you know. I can hold my own with just about anything you throw at me." Rachel stepped closer so no one could overhear her next words. "And that includes you, Rancher McCoy."

Rachel stepped away and Shivley couldn't move. Rachel's voice was seductive and her breath caressed her cheek when she confidently stated her parting words. Shively felt an overwhelming urge to run, but she didn't know in which direction. Should she run away from the temptation Rachel so self-assuredly offered or run toward the fulfillment she suspected she would find in her arms? She took the safe way out and simply watched the water fill the tank.

The sun was descending when Shivley stopped the herd. They had ridden all afternoon, driving the fifty head of cattle back to the confines of the ranch. Rachel was never far from her sight and Shivley was watching now as she sharply reined her horse to the left to keep a young calf from bolting.

Rachel didn't think, she simply reacted when she noticed the calf moving a split second before her horse. She was sore and tired from being in the saddle since the sun rose, but the ache in her muscles was a welcome respite to the endless, mind-numbing meetings that filled most of her days.

Rachel was looking forward to spending the night under

the stars. Well, not exactly under the stars. Ann had met them a few minutes earlier with the bed of the truck filled with tents for each woman and the supplies they would need for the remainder of the roundup. Rachel suspected the ground would be hard and the night air cool and had silently made a bet with herself as to which of her fellow guests would complain first. Her money was on Christina.

After a dinner of steaks perfectly grilled over the open fire, the women settled in around the campfire. The herd was bedded down for the night with Gail and Bart taking the first watch over their day's hard work. While the crickets chirped in the distance, Jane softly strummed on the guitar she had asked Ann to bring.

Shivley sat on a downed log, strong hands wrapped around her warm cup of coffee. Sue kept a running monologue going in her right ear, and Shivley was grateful the only thing required from her was an occasional nod. Her gaze kept drifting to Rachel sitting across from her. The light from the fire cast a warm glow on her face, and when their eyes met Shivley lost her breath. Dancing flames of desire mirrored those of their campfire.

The sound of her name caught her attention and Shivley asked, "I'm sorry. What did you say?"

Christina repeated her question. "I said it's your turn."

Shivley was at a loss as to what *turn* Christina was referring to. She hadn't been following the conversation. In fact, she hadn't heard a word anyone said in the last five minutes. "I'm sorry. My mind was somewhere else. What am I supposed to do?" She shot a glance at Rachel, whose expression told Shivley that she knew exactly where her mind had been.

"Your wildest fantasy. All of us except you and Rachel have bared our innermost sexual desires. You're up. And I for one am definitely interested."

Of that Shivley was certain. All day long, Christina had continued to let it be known in not so subtle ways that all Shivley needed to do was give her the word.

Rachel had been half listening to the trail of confessions offered up by her fellow guests, and they ranged from the sublime to the downright outrageous. Christina's well-rehearsed plan was specifically directed at Shivley but lost on their host's inattentiveness. Women like Christina didn't threaten Rachel. There was a fine line between letting a woman know you were interested and throwing yourself at her. To Rachel, if a woman was equally interested she would quickly pick up the familiar signs. Throwing yourself at somebody was simply unnecessary. Christina was definitely on the wrong side of that line.

Rachel joined in. "Yes, Shivley, tell us. What is your wildest sexual fantasy?" Her voice was low and husky, and Rachel saw Shivley's expression change from polite interest to want when she said the word *sexual*. Now she really wanted to know.

"What ever happened to ghost stories and singing songs around the campfire?" Shivley asked.

"That went out with spin the bottle," Jackie said.

"I kind of liked spin the bottle," Rachel mused.

Shivley rose to the challenge she saw in Rachel's eyes. "All right." She held Rachel's look but addressed her question to the other women. "Is this just fantasy in general or specific details?"

"Details," was the chorus of replies, along with a hoot or two to set the mood.

Shivley didn't have sexual fantasies, or at least none she would classify as fantasy, let alone wild ones. Fantasies were those things that were just at the tip of your fingers or were so far out of reach they would probably never come true. She wanted a woman to share her life with, simple as that. But she knew that was not what her guests were talking about, and she was all about giving her guests what they were looking for. She dragged her eyes away from Rachel.

"I'm not much of a kiss-and-tell kind of girl."

"Get over it." This time it was Sue who replied, and the other women cheered in agreement.

Shivley chuckled. "I can see I'm outnumbered here."

"Smart woman. Now cough it up," Jane said.

"Okay, okay, let me think. I have so many to choose from." She winked at Jane and took a breath. "I'm driving on a quiet road out in the middle of nowhere. Rod Stewart is singing his song about hot legs on the radio when I round the corner and there she is." Shivley hesitated and slowly turned her head and locked on Rachel's knowing eyes. "She's lost, and being the kindhearted soul that I am, I offer to help her find her way."

"You can show me the way anytime," Debra said teasingly and was rewarded with a jab in the side by her lover.

Shivley laughed. "I'll keep that in mind. Anyway, she has legs that go on forever in a pair of tight jeans, and of course since I am a red-blooded lesbian, the first thing I do is think about them wrapped around me." Several women echoed her thoughts. "She is the most beautiful, stunning, sexy woman I've ever seen, and my libido starts telling me I need to have her. She's holding a map and is standing very close to me. She smells like a warm spring day and all I want to do is feel the sun on my back and her under me."

"Better use sunscreen."

Shivley nodded in agreement. "Definitely, because I plan to be in that position for a long, long time." She grinned. "Anyway, her hands are shaking as she hands me the map.

I can't seem to focus on the lines and numbers because she has moved even closer and her body is practically touching me. Somehow I give her directions, and when she reaches for the map our fingers touch. We look at each other and we both know exactly what we want." Shivley made eye contact with each woman, saving Rachel for last.

Rachel's heart raced when she realized Shivley was talking about the first time they'd met. She held her breath wondering just how much Shivley would reveal about their first meeting. Was Shivley telling the truth or simply fiction for the sake of the discussion?

"She doesn't say a word but walks into the woods, and of course I follow her. Who gives a shit about our cars sitting in the middle of the road? My mouth waters as I watch her walking in front of me, and I can't wait to get my hands on her. She stops under a canopy of trees and turns around. Her eyes are blazing with lust and she slowly starts unbuttoning her shirt." Shivley looked to her left and right and every pair of eyes was on her, but the only ones she was interested in belonged to the woman in her fantasy.

"She drops her shirt from her shoulders and she's not wearing anything underneath. I can't move. I want to touch her, taste her, but I'm frozen right in that spot and can't move. She gives me a 'come and get me' look and reaches for the snap on her jeans." Shivley took a deep breath, regaining her equilibrium. She had just described what she wished had happened on that dirt road a few short days ago.

"And?" Sue asked for the group waiting expectantly for the rest of the story.

"And," Shivley hesitated before continuing, "and that's it. I told you I'm not the kiss-and-tell kind of girl. I tried, but I guess I can't get over it."

The group exploded in frustration and questions, and Rachel exhaled. She admitted that she was curious as to what would happen next, but also slightly relieved that she didn't have it played out in front of these strangers. Her mouth was dry and her heart was beating so loud she could barely hear Shivley's responses to the questions and pleadings from her trailmates.

"No, not anymore. I'm done." The hoots and hollers for more continued. "Now, ladies, I'm the trail boss, and remember I told you, the trail boss has the last word, or in this case two words. I'm done." Shivley desperately wanted to continue her fantasy, but only in the privacy of her tent and only with one woman.

Jane interrupted and let her off the hook. "Okay, Rachel, you're up. Your fantasy is the last one of the night, so you'd better make it good."

Rachel was jolted to attention at the sound of her name. When the women started playing the game of kiss and tell, she knew they wouldn't let her off the hook. Rachel was still so caught up in the sound of Shivley's voice and the look on her face as she'd told her fantasy that all she really wanted to do was act out what Shivley had described and add her own finishing touches. But instead she took a different spin on the truth.

"I want to live happily ever after."

"What?" Debra asked, confused.

"I want to live happily ever after."

"That's not a fantasy," Sue countered.

"In my world it is." Rachel's voice was soft and low and she spoke to the fire. She didn't have the childhood these women had. She'd never experienced hope, security, or a family. Rachel wasn't even sure she would know happily ever after if it kissed her right on the mouth.

Shivley was stunned by Rachel's declaration. She was expecting something vivid, wild, and probably slightly dangerous, but not this. Not something as simple as happiness. *But then again happiness has a unique definition for every person, and Rachel must want it very badly.*

CHAPTER TWENTY-ONE

One by one the women retreated to their tents and Shivley was left alone with Rachel beside the dwindling fire. She stirred the hot embers, feeling the heat rise. Her face was warm but her body was on fire. Rachel gave no indication she was ready to turn in, and they sat together under the stars without saying a word. The rustling inside the tents subsided and the silence was peppered with the sounds of the night; an owl hooted not far away.

There is no mistaking the sound of two women making love. Shivley cocked her head when the first soft moans drifted through the black night and settled around them. She glanced across the dying coals to find Rachel was looking right at her. The echo of mounting need hovered around them and Shivley fought the urge to close the short distance between them and take Rachel into her arms. She wanted Rachel, of that she was certain, and she silently cursed her sense of propriety or fear or whatever the hell was holding her back.

The throbbing between Rachel's legs increased in tempo along with the sounds coming from the tent thirty feet away. It had been months since Rachel had had sex, and the passion her co-wranglers were enjoying was making it anything but easy for her to sit calmly as if nothing were happening. *Why am I still sitting here and not over there?* Rachel didn't have an answer to her question. Their attraction was mutual and they were both single, Shivley had said as much.

The sound of muffled passion propelled Shivley into action. She stood on shaking legs and crossed the short distance, pulling Rachel to her feet all in one motion. She crushed Rachel to her, burying her hands in soft hair and pulling her mouth roughly against hers. Rachel responded instantly, deepening the kiss, and Shivley was overcome with hunger. Her tongue plundered Rachel's mouth while her hands roamed over the slight body leaning into hers. She was quickly losing control.

Rachel dragged her mouth away from Shivley's exploring tongue and took a deep breath. The look of unbridled lust in Shivley's eyes and the suddenness of her advance had taken her breath away. She filled her lungs with the scent of the cool summer night. Shivley smelled of pine trees and leather, and Rachel had a fleeting thought that she would make a fortune if she were ever able to bottle the scent. As it was, she was overwhelmed by the peacefulness of the bright stars twinkling overhead, to say nothing about Shivley's hands, which were enticingly close to her breasts. Mother Nature had provided the perfect ambience for a night of passion and Rachel was never more ready.

Rachel was rarely disappointed in the arms of a beautiful woman, in part because she was usually the one in charge and she chose partners who knew their way around a woman's body. Lust was never a problem, nor was achieving orgasm, but there was something about being in Shivley's arms that made Rachel want something more than sheer physical release. For the first time, she felt uneasy, almost as if she wouldn't know what to do. She didn't get a chance to worry when a loud crack of thunder exploded around them and Shivley tore herself out of her arms.

"The herd. They'll be spooked by this. We've all got to get back in the saddle." Shivley stepped away and started calling to the other women to get dressed and get their gear. She grabbed her saddle and ran to the picket line where the horses had been tied. In quiet tones she soothed the restless animals. It wouldn't do them any good if the horses bolted and left them with nothing other than Ann's pick-up.

Shivley heard the sound of movement behind her and turned just as Rachel was heaving her saddle onto the back of her horse. Rachel tightened the cinch and adjusted the reins without hesitation. Shivley untied the reins and jumped onto her mount a split second before Rachel. Rachel settled into the saddle and their eyes met. Unfulfilled desire was written all over Rachel's face and Shivley started to say something when she realized nothing really needed to be said.

"Let's go!" Shivley commanded. "You know what to do." It was more of a statement than a question. After four days in the saddle Shivley knew Rachel was an experienced horsewoman and wouldn't need any instructions.

Unfortunately, the other women didn't have a clue. Shivley had to give specific instructions several times to the women and was shorthanded when Joyce was so scared she would not come out of her tent. They spent the remainder of the stormy night circling the herd, trying to keep them from bolting in every direction. Finally, just before dawn, the storm passed and the women fell into their tents in complete exhaustion.

❖

Sweat slid down the center of her back when Rachel heaved another pitchfork of soiled straw out of the stall. She had been up since before dawn, unable to sleep, her thoughts a jumble of the roundup, the storm, and Shivley. They'd been too exhausted to say much of anything to each other as they rode the remaining distance back to the ranch the day before. Every muscle in her body ached and her hands were chapped from hours in wet gloves. Once the cattle were secured in the pen she stumbled up the stairs, and after a hot shower, collapsed on her bed, and slept right through dinner.

Shivley had not given any indication that mucking the stalls was the guests' responsibility, but Rachel's experience gave her the insight into what was required to run a ranch of this size. She needed the physical activity to clear her mind.

"You don't have to do that." Shivley had been standing in the doorway for several minutes watching Rachel rhythmically swing the pitchfork back and forth full of straw from the stall to the wheelbarrow, which was overflowing from her labors. She didn't know why Rachel was out here and had even less of a clue what she was using the activity to escape from. Whatever it was, was serious. Shivley had seen the same determination on Rachel's face the past few days as she expertly handled her horse, a rope, and now the pitchfork.

Rachel belonged on a ranch. The familiarity with which she walked around the stalls and the corrals, the way she knew her way around in the barn, and of course the way she sat her horse were all clearly indicative that there was someone very different than the Rachel Stanton everyone knew.

Rachel spun around, startled by the voice intruding on the quiet of the barn. Shivley was silhouetted in the doorway, the rising sun behind her obscuring her face. "I've been shoveling shit of one kind or another most of my life. Doesn't take much to find where it is and even less to get rid of it." If anyone was an expert about shoveling shit, it was Rachel. In the past ten years, she had been exposed to more half-truths, lies, and crap than the average person, and she was tired of it all.

The bitterness in Rachel's reply surprised Shivley, but what was more disconcerting was the stab of pain it caused in her chest. She didn't want Rachel to feel pain and she had an overwhelming need to ease her burden. "Yeah, but most people don't do anything to get rid of it. They either walk around it or ignore it."

"I'm afraid I don't have that luxury. My job is to make it disappear, or better yet make it appear as if it never happened, or at least didn't happen the way you think it did. Occupational hazard, I guess, that spills over into my personal life as well."

"And you're happy with that?"

Rachel finally broke the smooth cadence of her strokes she had maintained throughout the conversation. To the casual observer it might have gone unnoticed, but Shivley saw it loud and clear.

"It's what I do. And I'm damn good at it." And the balance in her bank account confirmed it. Rachel was known in the political power circles as the one to have on your team if you wanted to win, and win big. She was highly sought after by those on both sides of the political fence, having no allegiance to the politics of either one. She demanded and received big money for her talent and was booked several years into the future.

Shivley didn't miss the evasive answer that may have pacified some, but not her. "That's not what I asked."

Rachel was not surprised that her noncommittal answer did not end the subject. She stabbed another clump of soiled straw and sighed. She was so tired of watching to make sure that every word she said could not be misconstrued, used against her, or even worse, become the featured sound bite on the evening news. "No, it isn't, but that's my answer nonetheless." She knew she sounded harsh but was too tired to care.

"Rachel?"

Chills dashed down her spine the way Shivley spoke her name, and Rachel lost her focus, almost stabbing herself in the foot. She stopped and slowly turned to face Shivley. Shivley had not moved, and the distance between them felt like a crevasse and she was teetering on the edge, unsure whether to retreat or jump.

Shivley had come to talk with Rachel and almost lost her nerve when she saw the distress on her face. It was important and she pushed forward. "We need to talk." Rachel didn't reply but continued to look at her as if she were waiting for the opportunity to flee. "About the other night."

"All right." Rachel didn't know what else to say. She was afraid if she said anything it would be the wrong thing and Shivley would disappear, like all the other good things that had come her way. And she didn't want her to. She wanted to be in Shivley's arms today, tomorrow, and every day after that. And that scared her more than anything ever had before.

"What would have happened if the storm hadn't hit?" Shivley knew. She'd thought about it all day and dreamed about it all night.

Rachel propped the pitchfork against the nearest wall and wiped her hands nervously on her pants. "You tell me." In their previous interludes, Shivley had always been the one who pulled away. Rachel wondered if it would have been different, that night under the stars.

Shivley didn't bother with useless words, she simply closed the gap between them and took Rachel into her arms. She gazed into uncertain eyes and slowly lowered her head and kissed Rachel with a tenderness she had never felt before. She wanted to erase the pain that Rachel had buried deep under years of self-preservation.

Rachel wrapped her arms around Shivley's strong neck and stood on her toes, craving the feel of Shivley's body against her own. They had been together like this only a few times, but her body instantly remembered how it had felt and her mind reeled from the sensation. She felt safe. No harm would come to her while she was wrapped in Shivley's embrace. She had never felt this way with anyone before. While other children were blessed with this feeling in the arms of their parents and family, Rachel had not been. While other children felt loved every day of their lives, Rachel had not. But she did now, and she didn't want to let go.

Rachel dropped to the ground, pulling Shivley with her. The prickly hay against her back went unnoticed when Shivley settled on top of her. Shivley's tongue explored her mouth and Rachel slipped her hands under the soft work shirt. Shivley's muscles twitched under her fingers, and Rachel had to explore every inch of the quivering flesh. She started to unbutton Shivley's shirt but Shivley gently grasped her hands.

"Wait." Shivley could hardly think straight. "Not here, not like this." Her breath was rapid, and her head was spinning. She blinked several times to clear her head. "I want our first time to be perfect, on clean sheets in a soft bed, not in an old barn smelling like horses." She started to get up, but Rachel held her firmly in place.

Rachel had never felt a time or place more perfect than the one she was in right now. She had had sex with countless women in five-star hotels with plush carpet and the finest linen money could buy, but it was nothing compared to what she was experiencing now. Her nose tickled with the comforting smells of tack and fresh straw. It was as if it had awakened senses that were long dormant and reminded her of one of the few happy times in her life. "This is *exactly* where I want it to be." She pulled Shivley's lips to hers and lost herself in the kiss.

CHAPTER TWENTY-TWO

Shivley's hands shook so badly she could barely unbutton Rachel's shirt. She was out of practice in the art of undressing a woman, but she quickly dusted off her skills and Rachel's shirt fell open. She grinned.

Rachel's breasts were encased in a white bra, the top half covered in intricate lace patterns that barely covered the tanned flesh. Shivley's hand trembled as she lightly traced the outline of the pattern, Rachel's already erect nipples pushing even harder against the thin fabric.

"What are you grinning at?"

"I never expected a lacy bra under all this sweat and plain cotton shirt. A sports bra or a T-shirt, but never something like this. Very sexy." Shivley found the combination of butch and femme was indeed sexy. "Do you have matching panties?" The simple word "panties" conjured all kinds of images in Shivley's mind, and her mouth descended to the smooth flesh.

"You tell me." Rachel growled at the same time the buckle of her belt came loose. Overwhelmed by the need to touch

Shivley's skin, she pulled Shivley's shirt out of her pants and over her head.

Shivley lifted her head from the nipple she was teasing and once her shirt was off immediately returned and captured it with her teeth. The material was wet from her mouth and Rachel hissed and dug her fingernails into Shivley's back. Shivley's passion skyrocketed; she needed Rachel's skin against hers.

Shivley backed away and pulled Rachel into a sitting position. "I need to feel you. I need to taste you."

Rachel helped Shivley remove the rest of her shirt and she nibbled on Shivley's neck while Shivley unclasped her bra. Her breasts spilled out into Shivley's warm hands.

"My God, you're beautiful." Those were the only words that could even begin to adequately describe the vision in front of Shivley. Firm, full breasts rose and fell quickly, and she watched as Rachel's nipples hardened even more under her gaze. She was torn between wanting to continue feasting her eyes, or kissing every inch of them. Rachel made the decision for her.

The look of unbridled desire in Shivley's eyes was almost more than Rachel could bear. Reaching up, she put her hand behind Shivley's neck and pulled her to her aching breast. Shivley nibbled, which sent a signal straight to her clit, and if she was not careful, she would come right now. Rachel concentrated on opening the buckle on Shivley's belt and made short work of the buttons on her jeans.

Shivley's stomach quivered under her fingers and Rachel thrilled with the knowledge that Shivley was as turned on as she was. She teased her fingers across the top of the elastic band of Shivley's Jockeys and was rewarded with a low moan. Shivley switched to her other nipple and Rachel slid her fingers into wet warmth.

"My God, Shivley, you feel so good. Jesus." Rachel's fingers had been in a similar place with dozens of women, but none had ever been as soft and warm. She stroked Shivley softly, exploring the silky smoothness, intentionally staying away from her clit. She wanted to savor the moment when she first touched her.

Shivley's body was begging for release. She was way overdue for this. Rachel teased her unmercifully, and every time she came close to her clit, she would back away slightly as if she knew Shivley would explode at her first touch. Shivley dragged her mouth from the hard nipple and blazed a trail of nips and kisses up Rachel's neck. She slid her hand into Rachel's warmth the same time she slid her tongue into her mouth.

Rachel arched her back and opened her legs, allowing Shivley greater access. She mimicked the action of Shivley's hand in her pants and felt the impending orgasm start to creep down her spine.

"Are you sure you want to do this here, because in about two seconds I won't be able to stop," Shivley asked against her lips. Shivley wasn't even sure if she would be able to stop if Rachel asked her to.

Rachel was higher than she had ever been. Every nerve in her body was on fire, and she wanted Shivley more than she had wanted any woman. Rachel had done *this* in every conceivable position, and in some very risky places, but for the first time since her mother left she felt safe and wanted to lose herself in Shivley's arms. "Yes," was all she was able to say before she did.

Shivley felt as if she'd come home when Rachel shuddered in her arms. Rachel still had one hand in her pants, but the other held her tightly as she buried her face in Shivley's neck. Warm breath caressed Shivley's neck and drifted down her chest.

Shivley's hand filled with Rachel's desire, and she easily slipped her fingers inside. Rachel gasped and Shivley held her tighter. Slowly Shivley moved her fingers in and out, each time delving just a bit deeper until Rachel fully engulfed her. Rachel tossed her head back, and Shivley took advantage of the move and sank her teeth into the pulse point beating wildly on her smooth neck. Rachel's orgasm was quick and hard, and the muscles surrounding Shivley's fingers pulsated in rhythm with the tremors rocking her body.

Rachel blinked several times as the last shudder left her body. Her breathing was erratic and her limbs felt like lead, but she remained secure in Shivley's strong arms. The smell of hay penetrated her dazed senses, and little by little Rachel became aware of her surroundings. Shivley's heart beat rapidly against her chest and the throbbing under her fingers told her that Shivley was as aroused as she had been. Christ, as she still was. She was thrilled when Shivley's body reacted to the slightest movement of her hand.

And the slightest movement was all Shivley needed. She fought to remain in control, but Rachel coming in her arms not once but twice made her pent-up passion explode like a schoolboy on his first time. Spasm after spasm shook her body and stars burst behind her eyes in celebration. It had been so long since she'd experienced release in a woman's arms, and it was glorious. Rachel's fingers moved again and Shivley grasped her wrist tightly.

"No." She needed a minute to recover.

"But I'm not done with you yet." Rachel liked to give just as much as she liked to receive, but with Shivley what she was feeling was different. It wasn't the usual bravado of successfully bringing another woman to orgasm, it was something entirely unfamiliar. For the first time she was touched by the entire experience. It was more than simply sex, the physical reaction of two bodies. She was protective. Protective of Shivley in her arms. Protective of her emotions and her heart. She wanted to make Shivley happy. She started to say something, but Shivley put her finger over Rachel's mouth, signaling for her to be quiet.

"I don't know where she is. You check the rest of the barn and I'll look around back." It was Gail.

"She couldn't have gone far, the Jeep's still here," Bart replied.

Shivley quickly surveyed their surroundings and was relieved that they were far enough into the stall that they could not be seen by someone just walking by. Bart would have to enter the stall and turn right for them to be discovered. And how embarrassing would that be, with both of them naked from the waist up and Rachel's hand still down the front of her pants?

Rachel felt the tension in Shivley's body as Bart approached. She didn't move for fear of being heard or setting Shivley off again. She had been caught off guard when Shivley came so fast and she didn't have a chance to savor it; she was not about to let that happen again.

Seconds passed that felt like hours to Shivley before her hired hand walked the full length of the barn and out the east door. She breathed a sigh of relief and relaxed back into the pile of hay, Rachel's hand sliding out of her pants.

"That would have been awkward," Shivley murmured quietly.

Rachel sat up and looked down at Shivley, who had taken her so perfectly. She was beautiful. It wasn't just her physical beauty but her inner strength. She had almost single-handedly created this ranch, this escape from reality where Rachel had finally come home. She caressed Shivley's cheek with the back of her fingers. "One minute sooner and it would have been a little more than awkward." Rachel smiled.

"What are you smiling about?" Shivley turned her cheek into Rachel's palm.

"I was remembering the time Mrs. Stacey caught me and Kathy Simcox in the showers."

"In the showers. Jeez, don't you think that was a bit risky?"

"We were fifteen," Rachel replied as if that explained it.

"What did she say?"

Rachel chuckled. She could still hear Mrs. Stacey's stern voice. "Girls, surely you can find a more private place."

"What did you do?" Shivley was grateful she had never been caught in the act. High school was difficult enough without being caught having sex with a girl.

"We did as we were told. We found a more private place."

"Where's Kathy Simcox now?" Shivley could not believe she was having the kind of conversation you would have over coffee or lunch, not half dressed in a horse stall.

"Last I heard she was on her third husband and had gained fifty pounds." Rachel grimaced at the thought.

Shivley couldn't take her eyes off Rachel. She wanted to pull Rachel to her and touch her again and again and again. She knew what she had just experienced with Rachel was just the tip of the iceberg, and if she let herself, she could spend the rest of her life finding out. But this was not the time or the place to start down that path. "You are very beautiful, and as much as I'd like to continue this, preferably somewhere more comfortable, I need to see what they need. They won't stop looking until they find me."

"It's good to hear you want to continue this, because as I

said, I'm not through with you yet." Rachel's heart pounded when she thought of all the things she wanted to do to Shivley. It would take all night, if not a lifetime. Rachel stood on shaky legs and pulled Shivley to her feet. She gave Shivley a long, sensuous kiss, her pulse racing again. She made herself pull away before she lost control again.

Shivley helped Rachel back into her clothes but couldn't help lingering on her bra. Her fingers lightly skimmed over the delicate lace and her crotch throbbed remembering the feel of Rachel's breasts. She handed the delicate garment to Rachel and helped her hook the front closure. Shivley's hands shook as she buttoned her shirt. She stopped and looked over at Rachel. The morning sun streaked through the spaces between the boards of the wall, highlighting the gold in Rachel's hair. She reached out a quivering hand and touched the soft curls. They were like bands of silk flowing between her fingers, and Shivley looked deep into Rachel's eyes. "See you at breakfast?" Rachel nodded and Shivley swooped in for one last kiss and then walked out of the stall.

❖

They did see each other at breakfast and for just about every minute the rest of the day. Unfortunately, except for a few minutes after lunch, Rachel and Shivley were never alone. The morning had been spent separating the cattle they had brought in the day before, males in one pen, females in another. Next were shots, tagging, and general health inspection of the animals.

When they were finally alone, it was just outside the back door of the house. Rachel had watched Shivley go into the house and waited for her in the comfort of one of the chairs in the yard. Rachel had a difficult time concentrating on what she was doing this morning, their romp in the hay earlier only whetting her appetite. There was one moment when Shivley had tied the legs of one of the steers and Rachel imagined what it would be like if Shivley had her tied up like that. She had stumbled and almost fallen in a pile of cow shit and forced herself to pay attention from then on.

While Rachel waited anxiously for Shivley to exit, she wondered what her business associates would think if they could see her now. Her jeans were filthy, her T-shirt torn on one side, her hair was plastered to her head under her hat, and she had stepped in God knows what. And she had never felt so alive. In her job she had more power than she ever imagined and made more money than she could spend. Her clients dominated the American political scene. She had dined with heads of state and Wall Street bankers, and controlled the purse strings of tens of millions of dollars of campaign contributions. But nothing compared to how she felt right now sitting under a cloudless Arizona sky.

Her heart unexpectedly leapt at the sight of Shivley through the window. Rachel was typically calm and cool when it came to women, but all reason dissolved when Shivley stepped out the door. She practically threw herself into Shivley's arms and kissed her so passionately it left both of them struggling to breathe. Rachel couldn't get close enough. She wanted to be all over Shivley, to touch and feel and taste every inch of her. She wanted to be inside her. Not just her fingers or her mouth, but she actually wanted to crawl inside Shivley and never come out.

Shivley staggered backward from the momentum of Rachel in her arms. She was momentarily stunned by the intensity of Rachel's kiss, but then instinct took over and she returned it with equal abandon. Rachel's body responded to her wandering hands, and Shivley threatened to explode just from her kiss. She slid a thigh between Rachel's legs and Rachel immediately arched into it.

"You keep that up and I'm going to come," Rachel croaked between kisses.

"You started it," Shivley countered.

"Then you'd better finish it." Rachel shuddered when Shivley's hands snaked under her shirt. Her hands were those of a woman who worked with them day in and day out, rough calluses scratching sensuously over her bare skin. Shivley's touch was more delicate and exciting than any expensively manicured hand had ever been.

"Right here? Right now?" Shivley was holding on to her control by sheer willpower. She had not expected Rachel to be just outside the door and certainly hadn't expected what was happening right this minute. Rachel's eagerness was so exciting Shivley thought she would faint.

Rachel tensed, on the verge of orgasm. Shivley's tongue danced in and out of her mouth, matching the cadence her crotch was grinding into Shivley's thigh. She lost all coherent thought and didn't care. She needed this. Needed it just like this and even more. Her body and mind craved release. She was barely able to say, "Right now," before she exploded in a massive climax.

Shivley held her as wave after wave of orgasm rocked her body. Everything stopped except for the complete and utter feeling of coming home in Shivley's arms. She buried her face in Shivley's neck while flashes of red and yellow exploded behind her eyelids. She was floating, but the security of Shivley's arms was her safety net. Shivley held her tightly as her trembling subsided.

Shivley's back was pressed against the door, the knob digging into her back. Breathing heavily, she slowly lowered her leg, and Rachel moaned at the loss of contact. Shivley smoothed Rachel's shirt down, glancing over her shoulder, relieved they had not attracted an audience. Rachel's hot breath blew down the collar of her shirt. She hated to break the moment, but anyone could walk by at any time, causing them both considerable embarrassment.

"Rachel?"

"Mmm?" It was all Rachel could say. Her limbs were lethargic, her brain foggy, and her clit still pounding.

"Rachel, sweetie. Uh, we…uh…anyone could see us." Shivley scanned the yard again.

"Mmm, I don't care." Rachel was too content to recognize the endearment.

"I'll take that as a compliment, but we really need to… uh…" Shivley didn't know what to call what they needed to do. *Uncouple? Untangle? Step inside and do it on the kitchen table?* Rachel emitted a huge sigh, or an aftershock of her orgasm, Shivley wasn't sure which. She loosened her hold as Rachel put an inch between them.

"Oh my God, I have no idea where that came from." Rachel had never thrown herself at a woman as recklessly as she just had. She was out of control and had no idea when she crossed the line. She had never been so fully consumed by the need to be in the arms of a woman.

"I don't know, but I liked it." Shivley smiled, lifting Rachel's chin to look into her eyes. "Very much." Rachel blushed. Shivley could swear her heart skipped a beat.

"You liked it?" Rachel emphasized the word *you*. She was embarrassed by her complete abandon in Shivley's arms. It was so out of character for her to lose control like she had. She couldn't look Shivley in the eye, but the constant pressure on her chin encouraged her to. Shivley's eyes were warm, passionate, and full of acceptance.

"Yes. I did. And I'm going to have a difficult time

focusing this afternoon with a wet crotch and a severe hard-on. Thank God I'm not a guy." She chuckled. "Now *that* would be embarrassing." Rachel smiled, but Shivley read hesitation in her eyes. She wanted to make it disappear, and the only way she knew how was to kiss her. Rachel's eyes sparked as she lowered her head. Rachel's lips were still warm from their kisses and she started to spin with sensation again. Her senses were alive. Rachel in her arms, the warm sun on her face. She could kiss Rachel all day, but Lucy barking somewhere to her left brought her back to reality. She ended the kiss and slowly released her. Rachel's face was flushed and she looked a little dreamy. Shivley's hand was trembling when she cupped Rachel's check. She wanted to say something, anything, but she wasn't sure what. The words that came to mind scared her. Rachel would be leaving in three days.

❖

The sound of laughter filled the air when Shivley stepped out onto the patio. Becky, Ellen, and Christina had made a return appearance in the Jacuzzi after dinner, and this evening Rachel had joined them. Shivley noted the two empty bottles of wine on the bench along with several towels and three damp swimsuits. She didn't have a chance to guess which of the women remained clothed under the bubbles before Christina asked her to join them.

"It sounds tempting, but I'm afraid I have to pass tonight, ladies. I have a previous commitment." Shivley's answer was directed at Christina, but her eyes never left Rachel's.

"Anything I can give you a hand with?" Christina asked suggestively.

Shivley knew exactly what Christina was alluding to and she thought she saw a spark of…what? Jealousy in Rachel's eyes? She filed that thought away for future reference. She had not yet calmed down from their morning encounter in the barn when Rachel pounced on her after lunch. And now imagining the soft, warm flesh hiding under the bubbles of the jets was almost too much to bear.

"Actually, no. I promised I'd play poker with Debra, Jane, and Cindy. They needed a fourth and I volunteered."

"If it's strip poker, can I play?" Christina's voice was slightly slurred. All evening she had been drowning her disappointment over not getting into Shivley's sleeping bag.

"You already have your clothes off, Christina." Becky stated what was obvious.

"So what? So do you," Christina whined like a petulant child.

Shivley didn't have to do the math to know that there was a fifty-fifty chance that the remaining suit on the bench belonged to Rachel. She squinted harder at the water, deciding there was a far greater probability it belonged to Ellen. After all, if one of the partners was relaxing in the buff, why wouldn't the other be as well?

"I don't think it's strip poker, Christina, but if anyone mentions it I'll let you know." Shivley slowly walked past the side of the Jacuzzi where Rachel sat up to her neck in water. She didn't see any signs of swimsuit straps across Rachel's tanned shoulders or around her neck, and she prayed she wouldn't fall all over herself on the way past.

"I'd like to see her naked," Christina wished out loud to Shivley's departing back.

"Who? The boss lady?" Ellen had given Shivley the nickname soon after they had all met that first day.

"Oh, yeah. She can boss me around anytime." Christina took a long swallow of her wine, licking her lips as if imagining they tasted like Shivley.

"She's way out of your league, girl," Becky commented.

"Why do you say that?" Christina's words had begun to slur more noticeably.

"You've been sniffing after her since the minute we landed, and she hasn't given you a second glance. I'm no Dear Abby, but I'd say she's not interested," Becky said by way of explanation.

Christina set her drink on the ledge and stood, water dripping off various mounds and curves of her perfect naked body. "She just hasn't seen what I've got to offer." Christina looked at each woman as if to say, "*Hello,* here it is."

Rachel squirmed on the hard fiberglass seat. Christina was twenty-five years old with large, firm breasts, a flat stomach, and a perfectly manicured bush, all above muscular thighs that Rachel thought could probably choke the breath out of you if they wrapped too tightly around you.

Christina dropped back into the water. "She's just hot. I mean, have you seen the way she rides her horse? I'd like her to ride me like that. Can you imagine what she'd be like in the sack? I bet she'd be the best lay you've ever had. Fifty bucks says I'm between her legs before this little vacation is over." Christina hadn't directed her bet to any one of the women in particular, and her voice carried just enough young cockiness to make you think she could really do it.

Rachel had heard enough. Between her stirred-up libido and the unexpected visit from Shivley moments earlier, she was wound tight as a drum. "Christina, shut the fuck up."

Three sets of eyes turned her way. Up until this point, other than hello, Rachel had said very little. "I can't speak for Becky and Ellen here, but I for one don't want to hear about your sexual conquests, especially if they involve our host." Rachel was surprised that she felt that way. She had competed for the same woman before and occasionally lost, but rarely gave it a second thought. Rachel wondered why she didn't like the possibility of someone else touching Shivley.

"Ooh, touchy, touchy, are we? Maybe you want a little bit for yourself. Or maybe you want all of it."

Christina was drunk and Rachel was not in the mood to argue or even drown her, for that matter. "Jesus, Christina, you sound exactly like a man. Shivley is probably more than just a good fuck and you should treat her with a little respect. Obviously she's intelligent and capable. She has this ranch, for Christ's sake. She knows what she's doing and is successful doing it. Yes, she's attractive, and I'm sure more women than not would want to get into her pants, but isn't that a bit superficial?" Rachel stopped when she realized she was beginning to sound like a hypocrite. Hadn't that always been what she was interested in?

Christina refilled her glass. "Who cares? She's hot and I'm horny. Sounds like a match made in heaven to me."

❖

Rachel wrapped the robe tighter around herself to ward off the chill from her wet body and walked through the kitchen to the great room. The poker players were sitting around a circular table covered in felt that dampened the clinking of chips as they hit the table. Beer bottles were scattered at their feet and the smell of popcorn filled the air. Every player was studying the cards in her hand with intense concentration as if it were the final hand in the World Series of Poker. Every player except Shivley.

The stacks of chips in front of Shivley were much larger than everyone else's, and she wore a corresponding satisfied expression on her face. She leaned back with a relaxed air that reminded Rachel of the characters in *Butch Cassidy and the*

Sundance Kid. Rachel was a killer poker player, having spent many days and nights playing the game to pass the time on buses or airplanes while on the campaign trail. Debra grunted and tossed her cards face down on the table, the universal symbol of giving up any chance of winning the hand. Cindy soon followed, leaving Shivley and Jane to battle for the pile of chips between them. Rachel watched as Shivley stroked her cards gently, and she swore she could feel those fingers stroking her as skillfully as they did that morning. She shook her head to clear the image, but it was too late. Four cards and eight chips later, Cindy's fate was sealed and Shivley gathered the chips toward her.

"Another hand, ladies?" Shivley shuffled the deck.

"Are you crazy? You've taken every penny I have. I thought I was the guest, and as the guest you should let me win," Debra teased.

Shivley laughed. "Tsk, tsk. Somebody didn't read the fine print on the contract." All four women laughed and the sound of Rachel joining in pulled Shivley's attention away from the table.

"Enjoy the water?" A pair of dark legs peeked out at Shivley from under the white fluffy robe. Her pulse began to pound as she imagined Rachel stepping out of the Jacuzzi, warm water sliding down her body unimpeded by clothing.

"Not nearly as much as you seem to have enjoyed yourself. It looks like you cleaned their clocks." Rachel motioned to Shivley's winnings.

"She's a card shark," Jane said.

"And a damn good bluffer, too," Cindy added.

"Now, ladies," Shivley began, "you were the ones who invited me to your friendly little game. I just joined you to be polite." She mockingly defended her honor.

"Bullshit," Debra said and pushed herself away from the

table. "I demand a rematch. I'm not going to let you disappear with my two dollars and eighty cents without having the chance to win it back. I have rent to pay." She pointed her finger at Shivley and pretended to be angry and threatening. "I'll see you tomorrow, missy."

"Not me. If I lose any more Sue will kill me. It's my turn to buy the magazine at the airport for our return flight." Cindy laughed at her own joke and disappeared in the direction of the stairs, Jane following behind her.

Shivley and Rachel were the only ones left in the room. "You're not a very good hostess. Taking the milk money from those poor, innocent women. You ought to be ashamed of yourself." Rachel could barely contain her laughter.

"My mama always taught me to take advantage of every opportunity that came my way, and that includes women who don't know enough not to *bet* the milk money." Shivley was enjoying the light teasing between them. She had insisted on penny poker and she had won less than six dollars in the game.

Rachel stepped closer. Her heart pounded in her chest and her pulse throbbed between her legs as she closed the gap between them. The top of the robe slipped open and Shivley's eyes flashed with desire at the exposed flesh. Unlike the other women in the Jacuzzi, Rachel had kept her suit on while in the water, but she had removed it once she was out and toweled dry. Her breasts were bare underneath the robe, and her breathing quickened at Shivley's reaction to her nakedness.

Shivley fought her desire, her mind trying to remind her body that Rachel was leaving in a few days. She wasn't concerned with falling madly in love with her, but she wanted her more than she had ever wanted a woman before. As she struggled to maintain control, Rachel added more fuel to the fire. Slowly she untied the robe and let the belt fall to the floor.

The robe opened with each step she took, and in a moment she was standing within arm's reach of Shivley. Shivley's chest rocked up and down, her breathing shallow and coming in short bursts. This was the first time she had seen Rachel naked, and she was absolutely beautiful. Her neck was long and elegant, following down to breasts that fit perfectly in the palm of Shivley's hands. Her stomach was flat, with just a hint of an appendectomy scar just below and to the right of her belly button. Shivley's hand twitched as she anticipated the feeling of her fingers in the soft, downy hair between her legs.

Her mouth watered in anticipation. Rachel's body was breathtaking, with just the right amount of flesh filling out the curves that made her a very attractive woman. Shivley remembered the salty taste of Rachel in her mouth, and she unconsciously leaned forward to sample it again.

Rachel felt powerful, and as she watched Shivley respond to her, a feeling familiar yet unknown gripped her. With previous lovers she was usually the one in charge, and whether it was the result of her skill in seduction or too much alcohol intake by her partner, her partner always surrendered to her. But at this very moment, something felt different, very different. She wanted to lose control.

CHAPTER TWENTY-THREE

Rachel rationalized and blamed the feeling on the effects of thirty minutes in the hot tub. She suspected she was dehydrated from the day's activities and attributed her light-headedness to the wine she had with dinner. It absolutely had nothing to do with the look of unbridled desire emanating from Shivley, still seated in the chair. Her hand shook when she reached out and touched soft wavy hair. Her eyes never left Shivley's as she ran her fingers through the curls and around to the back of her head. She bent her head at the same time she pulled Shivley to her.

Shivley didn't hear anything except the pounding in her ears and could only see Rachel's mouth descending toward hers. Her mind screamed for her to stop what was sure to happen, but her body was focused solely on quenching the desire that raged through her. She let herself be drawn into a kiss that was soft yet insistent.

Shivley remained still as Rachel explored, alternately nibbling and sucking on her lips and the edges of her mouth with soft butterfly kisses. Again, Rachel asked and Shivley granted her permission to enter, and in an instant, tongues were battling for control. She pulled Rachel onto her lap and slid her hands under the material of the robe gliding smoothly along Rachel's silky skin. Her back was warm, and she traced the muscles and rib cage with alternating firm and feather-light caresses. Shivley's passion overtook her and she tore her mouth away from Rachel's and dragged it across the salty skin of her neck.

Rachel arched her neck, giving Shivley free access that she took without hesitation. She pulled Rachel closer and ran her tongue sensuously up and down the muscles quivering under her caresses. The feel of Rachel in her arms and the smell of her body permeated her consciousness.

A low moan escaped from Rachel's lips and she wrapped her arms around Shivley's neck, drawing them even closer. Her nipples leaped to attention when they made contact with Shivley's soft shirt. A jolt of desire shot through Rachel and cool air met the warm wetness between her exposed legs as she straddled Shivley's thighs. She needed to be touched, and most importantly, she wanted Shivley to touch her.

Shivley slid her hands between them and gently cupped one firm breast, then the other as her mouth left a trail of wet kisses from Rachel's neck to the peak of an erect nipple. She pointed her tongue and slowly circled the outer edges, fully exploring the taste and texture before capturing it in her mouth. She sucked lightly, continuing to circle the nipple with her tongue. Rachel trembled in her arms and Shivley took that as an invitation to continue. She turned her attention to Rachel's other breast, repeating the same slow, sensuous actions she had bestowed on the first.

Rachel was overwhelmed with sensation. Countless women had done exactly what Shivley was doing, but she could not remember ever being so aroused. She held Shivley's head to her breast and thrust her hips.

Shivley sensed Rachel's need and slid her hands slowly down her sides, her mouth never leaving the nipple. She flicked the hard pebble with her tongue. Rachel's hips moved in anticipation of her touch, and she couldn't wait any longer.

"Rachel, we can't do this here." Shivley didn't want to stop, but for the third time that day, they ran the risk of being caught in a compromising position.

"I can and I want to." It was all Rachel was able to say. Shivley's hands and tongue had made her lose focus.

Shivley removed her hands and pulled the front of Rachel's robe together. The backs of her knuckles lay against rock-hard nipples. She sighed deeply, trying to clear her head of the passion that made her dizzy. She looked into eyes that mirrored what she was feeling. "I don't doubt it, but that's not what I want." Shivley was serious now. "I need more than a quickie this time. I want to touch every inch of you without clothes or robes or anything else in the way. I want to feel your body tremble under my fingers. I want to feel you under me, your body singing with sensation. I need you naked in my bed with absolutely nothing between us. That's what I want. Nothing less."

The way that Shivley described her desire was, in a way, a declaration. She hadn't realized it when she said it but she wanted, she *needed*, Rachel in her life. Having her in her bed without that would be hollow. She hoped she had not scared Rachel away.

"I want that, too," Rachel whispered. She wanted more than another mindless, almost effortless fuck. She ached to connect with Shivley and to be deeply touched in return. Her life was shallow and superficial and she had found what she was looking for in Shivley's arms. She was terrified, but she knew that if she missed this opportunity, she would never have another.

They walked silently up the wide stairs. The thick carpet in the hall muffled Shivley's boots and the soft click of the latch of her bedroom door was the only sound in the house. Shivley pushed the lock in and the sound echoed in her ears. She turned on a small light sitting next to the clock on the nightstand. A soft pink glow cascaded over the king-size bed. Shivley turned and was stunned by Rachel's beauty.

Rachel slid the robe off her shoulders with agonizing slowness. But before she did Shivley saw a glint of fear in her eyes. It was so fleeting, Shivley wasn't certain she had seen it at all. Inch by inch Rachel revealed more skin, and Shivley could only stare. Rachel was perfect, from her strong shoulders to the tips of her pedicured toes and every inch between.

"You said something about being naked in your bed with nothing between us?" The way Shivley was looking at her was heady. It had been a long time since a woman had seen her absolutely naked like this. Usually they were between the sheets minutes after entering a room. Heat rushed through her body under Shivley's adoring gaze. She believed Shivley when she had said she was worth more than a casual fuck. No one had ever said that to her, and if they had she would have passed it off as a line.

But not this time. Not tonight. Rachel had become a different woman here on the ranch, and she realized that difference included how she would make love with Shivley. She wanted to be tender and gentle. Free to bond with Shivley in a way she never thought possible. She wanted Shivley, her rancher.

Shivley reached out her hand. It was more than a signal. It was an invitation. An invitation for Rachel to come to her. To join her in their lovemaking. It wasn't about one taking the other, but sharing of not just a physical but an emotional event as well. Rachel hesitated, and for a moment Shivley thought she might bolt.

Rachel almost did run. The last five minutes had been unlike any she had ever experienced. She knew what was happening, what Shivley was saying without a word. She had never been asked and she wasn't sure what her answer should be. She had no frame of reference for this. She had no idea what to do, what to say, or how to act. She was petrified. She looked into Shivley's eyes. She couldn't find the words to describe what was reflecting back at her, but she knew that she didn't see pride or the thrill of pending conquest. She stepped forward into more than Shivley's arms.

Shivley's gentle kiss lasted a lifetime. Rachel swayed into her, wrapping her arms tightly around her neck. Shivley's clothes were rough on her naked skin and only added to her awareness of who she was with. Shivley was solid, real, and everything Rachel would ever need.

Rachel's hands shook as she unbuttoned Shivley's shirt, and Shivley could hardly wait to feel Rachel naked against her. She deepened the kiss and shivered when Rachel slid the shirt off her shoulders and tossed it somewhere behind her. She broke the kiss for the second it took for Rachel to pull Shivley's T-shirt over her head, her lips lost until they could reclaim Rachel's once again.

The backs of Rachel's fingers pressed against Shivley's stomach as she made short work of her belt buckle. The metal tip clicked several times as it slid through the loops on the belt, sending a chill of excitement slashing through her. The sound of clothes deliberately coming off in preparation for love was thrilling. She helped Rachel remove her jeans and boots. They were both naked, free of any pretense, motionless in anticipation.

Time seemed to stand still for Rachel. She was lost in the depths of Shivley's eyes and the moment. She didn't know if they stood there for a minute or an hour, and it didn't matter when Shivley finally took her in her arms and laid her on her bed.

The sheets against Rachel's back were crisp and cool. They smelled like sunshine, fresh air, and Shivley. Shivley hovered above her, burning a trail over her body with her eyes. Ever so slowly she lowered her body until Rachel embraced Shivley's weight and wrapped her arms around her. Shivley moaned deeply in her ear. "My God, you feel good."

The sensation of Shivley's body on top of hers was overwhelming. They fit together perfectly, and Rachel savored the wonder of the first time. She wanted to embed this feeling in her memory to last a lifetime. Her hands drifted up and down Shivley's back, alternating between tickling soft skin and raking her fingernails over hard muscles. Shivley began to move in response to her seductive strokes and Rachel grew bolder.

Shivley shifted slightly, giving her better access to Rachel's body. She cradled Rachel's head in the crook of her elbow while her hand roamed freely over Rachel's soft body. Rachel pulled her head down and Shivley kissed her. Rachel's hands tangled in her hair, demanding more, and Shivley opened her mouth and deepened the kiss. She stroked a firm thigh and calf, lightly brushing the inside of her legs on the way back up to cup a full breast. Rachel bent her leg and wrapped it around Shivley's, pinning her tightly.

Shivley tore her mouth away and bent to nibble on first one breast, then its twin, each time starting on the outer edges and working toward the center where an erect nipple eagerly waited for her attention. Minute after minute, she feasted on Rachel's breasts while her hand drew teasingly closer to

Rachel's sweet spot. Rachel arched closer each time Shivley came anywhere near the area that was wet with desire.

Rachel couldn't stand it any longer. She grabbed Shivley's hand and thrust it between her legs. She felt Shivley stiffen and Rachel froze. What had she done?

"Shh, not so fast, sweetheart," Shivley offered in comfort. "I want you just as bad, but I want to go slow. We need to go slow. I want to learn your body, not just what to do to get you there," she said between wandering kisses.

Rachel relaxed but was unable to speak. Shivley had tormented her long enough and what she needed was release, but she would do this for Shivley because she wanted it. Her lover wanted it and she would not let her down.

Minutes of torment turned into hours of pleasure and Shivley drove her crazy with ecstasy, taking her higher and higher until she thought she might soar off into the night if she was unable to release the pressure that was building inside her. Finally Shivley shifted and kissed her way down her belly with agonizing slowness. Rachel could hardly breathe, her excitement was so great. She spread her legs in anticipation, but nothing had prepared her for this. Shivley's tongue was soft and gentle as it explored her folds, each stroke more confident than the last. The tip of Shivley's tongue lightly flicked over her clit and Rachel arched off the bed.

"Not yet," Shivley murmured against her. "I want to taste you, all of you."

Rachel struggled for control. She counted to ten, then forty, and felt her impending climax slowly drift away, but it was lingering not too far from the surface. She gripped the sheets in her sweaty palms, crushing them into tight clumps of blue cotton in her fists. Shivley's hands were under her cheeks, lifting her higher and higher into her mouth. Rachel was teetering on the precipice of the most powerful orgasm of her life. Not only did she want this, need this, but she was giving it to Shivley as well.

She celebrated her orgasm by calling Shivley's name into the night. She drifted out of consciousness at the pinnacle only to float back to reality to climax again and again. Wave after wave of pleasure crested over her, spilling into Shivley's mouth. Her breath came in gasps, and more than once she thought she would pass out from the pleasure.

Rachel had no idea how much time had passed when she finally opened her eyes. The blades of the ceiling fan were spinning silently above her, casting soft shadows across the walls. For a moment she didn't know where she was. *Shivley.* That one word said it all. Lifting her head slightly, she saw that Shivley was resting on the inside of her thigh, a small smile on her lips. *My God!* Rachel shuddered with an aftershock. Shivley's smile deepened.

"You're back," Shivley said softly. She had watched as Rachel approached climax and rode the crest for what seemed like an eternity. She had never seen a more beautiful sight and never tasted anything as sweet as Rachel coming for her. She wanted Rachel to stay in that perfect place and to never have to return.

"I don't know where you went, but the look of rapture on your face was absolutely beautiful." Rachel turned her eyes away and blushed. Shivley untangled herself from Rachel's legs and slowly crawled up Rachel's body once again. She kissed her tenderly and Rachel immediately put her arms around her and held her tight.

"God, you're beautiful," Shivley murmured against Rachel's neck.

"I don't know what to say." Rachel was in another time and another place. It was as if she was in a foreign country and didn't speak the language, didn't know what to do next or what was expected of her. Shivley kissed her throat, nibbled on her ear, and finally kissed her on the mouth.

Rachel's lips were swollen from their kisses, but they were still as soft as the first time Shivley had kissed her. She felt her desire rise again and lifted her head to look deeply into eyes mixed with wonder.

"You don't have to say anything. You already did." Rachel's body spoke volumes, as if turning every page in the book of her life. It told her every story, every thought, and every desire.

Rachel chuckled, slightly embarrassed by what Shivley was implying. She was typically not very vocal in bed, and she was afraid of just what she might have said. "Let's hope the others sleep soundly."

Shivley kissed her nose, a crooked smile on her face. "I hope so, too, because I've only just gotten started." She lowered her head again, fully intending to spend even longer discovering Rachel's body this time. An earsplitting crack drowned out Rachel's reply, and Shivley practically flew out of bed, almost spilling Rachel to the floor.

"What was that?" Rachel asked, looking around.

"I don't know, but it didn't sound good," Shivley replied, reaching for her clothes. She stopped suddenly and looked at Rachel as if asking permission to leave.

Rachel was touched that Shivley cared enough about her to not simply dash out and leave her hanging after such a beautiful moment. "It's okay. Go see what happened." She was rewarded with a wink and a quick kiss on the lips.

❖

"What are you doing out here?" Shivley asked, leading Midnight out of her stall. After leaving Rachel and stumbling into her clothes, she had quickly checked the interior of the house and found nothing amiss, then grabbed the flashlight off the counter by the back door and headed toward the barn. Her instinct was right, and as she stepped inside, she immediately sensed something terribly wrong. The horses were agitated, the tension in the air palpable. She checked each horse as she walked down the wide corridor and stopped when she got to Jasmine's stall. The gate was just as she had checked it earlier, but the stall was empty. A gaping hole in the rear was the exit point for the horse, and when Shivley stepped closer, there was evidence Jasmine had cut herself on the jagged wood on her way out. Obviously something terrible had frightened the horse enough for her to kick out the wall and bolt into the night.

"I'm coming with you," Rachel replied, tossing her saddle onto her horse. She reached under Bonanza's stomach, grabbed the billet, and pulled it through the buckle, cinching it tightly.

"No, you're not."

"Yes, I am." Rachel dropped the stirrup into position and threw the reins over Bonanza's neck.

"No, Rachel, you're not." Shivley was not about to let her track a runaway horse in the middle of the night.

"Shivley, I know what I'm doing. I can help." As Rachel had entered the barn a few minutes ago, she didn't need an engineering degree to figure out what had happened.

"Rachel, you are not going." Shivley accentuated every word. Her hands were on her hips and her feet spread apart as if preparing for battle.

Rachel remained calm. Shivley needed her help and she wasn't about to be pushed aside. Especially now, after what they had just shared. "And why is that?"

"This isn't your responsibility. You're a guest. You could get hurt."

"What?" Rachel was stunned.

"You heard me. Go on to bed." Shivley raised her leg to step into her stirrup. Rachel grabbed her arm and stopped her.

"A guest? I'm a guest? I can't believe you just said that." Rachel was hurt to think that Shivley considered her little more than a guest. She hesitated a moment to let her words sink in. She shook off the feeling, not about to let it discourage her. She ran her hand down Shivley's arm. "Shivley, I know what I'm doing," Rachel repeated. "And you know it, too." Rachel stood her ground as Shivley processed what she had just said.

Rachel's accusation pierced Shivley's focus on getting out and finding Jasmine. She almost doubled over from the twisting knife in her stomach. Rachel was much more than simply a guest. She was here with her now, in the middle of the night, without reservation or concern for her own safety. It was in that moment that Shivley fell in love with Rachel Stanton. Her heart raced, and there was nothing in the world other than the woman standing in front of her. Her T-shirt was inside out, the sleeves of her shirt were haphazardly rolled halfway up her forearms, and her hat was slightly askew on her head. And she was the most amazing woman Shivley had ever seen.

Midnight snorted next to her ear and Shivley's attention returned to her escaped horse. Rachel was not a novice, and she could use the help. But it was dangerous. Riding a horse in the dark was risky, and the last thing she wanted was for Rachel to get hurt. She opened her mouth to repeat her decision and just the opposite came out.

"Grab a flashlight and stay near me," she offered as an olive branch. Rachel held up the Maglite in her hand and Shivley shook her head. *Unbelievable.* Shivley pointed at Rachel and said, "And no heroics." She was rewarded with Rachel's smile.

The women rode into the dark night, their flashlights

illuminating the way. Rachel had no idea where they were headed, but Shivley seemed to have a sixth sense of which way Jasmine might have gone. They rode for an hour in silence.

"Has she run off before?"

Rachel's quiet voice penetrated the darkness that was settling around Shivley's heart. "No, never. There were some mountain lion tracks just outside her stall. One must have come down for some reason and spooked her."

"A mountain lion? Up here?" Rachel realized her question was stupid. She had no idea what wild animals roamed the countryside surrounding the ranch.

"They usually don't bother us. Something must have set this one off. I'm surprised I didn't hear any of the other horses. I'm sure there was a lot of commotion. I'm even more surprised that no one else heard it, either." Shivley frowned. She heard Rachel chuckle.

"What?" She turned to look at Rachel but could only see the outline of her face in the reflection of the flashlight.

"Well, we were, uh, kinda preoccupied," Rachel stammered. Shivley's head was trapped between her thighs at the time, so it was no wonder she didn't hear anything. Rachel was so transfixed the house could have collapsed around them and she wouldn't have noticed. Who knew about the other women, and frankly, they were the last thing on her mind.

Shivley was grateful that the darkness hid the embarrassment she felt rising to her cheeks. Of course there was absolutely no reason to be, but she was nonetheless. "I don't really know what to say to that."

"Well, if I were asked, I would say that it was the most exquisite experience I've ever had. Your hands knew just where to go and your fingers are very talented. And I won't even begin to talk about what your mouth can do." Rachel shuddered slightly after her last comment.

Shivley wanted Rachel again. Truth was, she had never stopped wanting her, but had pushed it aside when she realized Jasmine was missing. "Jeez, Rachel, I'm on the back of a horse here." She smiled. "You keep talking like that and I'm likely to fall off. Can we change the subject?"

Rachel's panties were soaked, and sitting astride her powerful horse in a rocking rhythm next to the woman responsible was all the encouragement she needed to agree. "Let's. Otherwise I might not be responsible for my actions." As much as she wanted to continue this conversation, she obligingly changed the subject. "Tell me about Jasmine."

Shivley was as disappointed as she was relieved, but she needed to concentrate on what they were doing right now. Shivley told Rachel how she and Dale would go riding a few times a month at a stable not far from their home. Dale was not a horsewoman. In fact, two thousand pounds of flesh actually made her nervous, but she knew how much Shivley loved riding and she would go with her. However, the only horse she would ride was Jasmine. When Shivley had bought the ranch, she bought Jasmine in memory of Dale, and the horse would always have a special place in her heart. She watched Rachel's reaction to her story and was relieved when all she saw was understanding.

Shivley turned her head, the smell of blood permeating the still air. Midnight smelled it at the same time, her ears perking up, her steps agitated. The beam from the strong flashlight shook slightly as it crisscrossed the ground twenty feet in front of them. Suddenly Shivley reined in her horse and trained the light on a dark pile off to the left of the trail. She swallowed bile and swung her leg over the saddle. "Shit."

Jasmine lay on her side with several large, jagged tears in her neck. Blood oozed from her injury and had spread on the ground around the mare's head. Her breathing was labored, and when Shivley shone the light in her eyes, they were glassy and dull.

"Oh, Jasmine," Shivley cried kneeling and cradling the horse's head in her lap. "Rachel, bring the first—" She didn't have to finish. Rachel was running toward her with the large red bag in her hand.

They worked together trying to stanch the bleeding, but the wounds were simply too great. Shivley sat back on her heels, looking at the mare, tears trickling down her cheek. Rachel knelt beside her, not saying a word. Shivley stroked Jasmine's face as she struggled to breathe. She bent down close to Jasmine's ear. "I love you." She kissed her on the nose and slowly stood again, not saying a word as she walked by Rachel. Shivley pulled the rifle she always carried from the scabbard and returned to where the horse lay.

Rachel stood as Shivley approached with the rifle in her hand. She knew there was no choice but to put the horse down; her injuries were too severe. It was the humane thing to do, and as she watched Shivley pull the trigger, her heart broke. It broke over the death of a wonderful animal and shattered for the pain Shivley must be feeling.

CHAPTER TWENTY-FOUR

The ride back to the ranch felt like an eternity. The only sound filling the quiet night was the soft thud of their horses' hooves striking the ground. With each step her horse took, Shivley felt that much more removed from Dale. In the beginning, Jasmine was her connection to Dale, but over the years she knew she was just feeling what she thought she was supposed to feel, not what she truly felt. She knew at the time it was ridiculous, and it was even more ridiculous now. Jasmine was a horse, but a horse she loved just the same, and along with that came the pain of losing her. She was grateful that Rachel didn't try to fill the silence with patronizing comments or conversation designed to make her feel better. Rachel seemed to know that Shivley needed her space and time to grieve. The lights of the ranch flickered into view as they rode closer.

They unsaddled their horses and secured their tack. On the long ride back, Rachel had no idea what to say to comfort her lover, so she had said nothing. Her heart ached for Shivley. She wanted to make the pain go away, she wanted to see her smile and hear her laugh again, but she knew it would take time. Time heals all wounds, the saying goes, but Rachel had anything but time left at the ranch.

"Shivley, I'm so sorry." Rachel stepped forward to comfort Shivley, who moved away from her.

"No, I'm a mess." *Physically and emotionally.*

Rachel was not deterred by the blood and took Shivley's hand. "Come on," she said, gently pulling her toward the house. "Let's get cleaned up. We both need a hot shower and some sleep." Shivley didn't protest as she led them across the yard, into the house, and into Shivley's bedroom.

Once inside the bathroom, Rachel released her hand and turned on the shower. Shivley was struggling with the buttons on her shirt and Rachel brushed her hands aside and finished the job. She removed Shivley's soiled clothes and tossed them into the adjacent laundry hamper. She stripped and led them both into the steaming water.

The spray of hot water pummeled Shivley's tired body and numbed mind. She stood under the flow like a statue as the blood and dirt sluiced off her body into a puddle at her feet before slipping down the drain. Before long Rachel's hands were covered with soap, and she slowly cleaned Shivley's back while massaging her tense muscles. Shivley was too tired to do anything other than stand there and be taken care of. It had been so long since someone had taken care of her.

"God, I'm tired," she thought out loud.

"Shh, just relax."

Rachel's hands were soft and gentle as they erased the mud and muck from her skin. There were only a few hours until dawn, and Shivley knew she needed to sleep, but Rachel's wandering hands had her body wanting to do other things. One minute she was dead tired and the next she was so aroused she could barely stand it. Rachel turned her around and began washing her chest and stomach. Shivley knew her ministrations were purely medicinal, but when Rachel's soapy palms circled her breast, she exploded.

Rachel reveled in the sensation of the hard body beneath her hands. She memorized every detail of muscles and skin as she gently washed away any physical trace of their ordeal. Rachel sensed that Shivley had been emotionally affected by having to kill one of her horses, and she knew firsthand that it took much longer to cleanse emotional wounds. Rachel's hands shook as she held Shivley's, carefully washing each finger. She had never felt so helpless with a woman before.

Rachel was not expecting it when Shivley spun them both around and pinned her to the shower wall. Shivley kissed her hard, and Rachel immediately responded. Her nipples hardened against Shivley's chest an instant before Shivley covered her mouth with hers. Shivley's tongue was insistent on entering her mouth and Rachel eagerly obliged. Shivley growled when Rachel slid her thigh high between her legs.

God damn, that feels good. Shivley almost lost control when Rachel reached between them and tweaked her nipples. There had always been a direct connection between her nipples and her clit, and the link was definitely still in place. She didn't know which sensation to concentrate on first. She cupped Rachel's butt in her hands and pulled her closer, increasing the friction on Rachel's thigh at the same time.

Rachel read Shivley's body language and felt her clit grow hard against her leg. She increased the pressure on Shivley's nipples and darted her tongue in and out of her mouth, mirroring the rhythm of Shivley rocking on her leg. Rachel felt powerful. She had the ability to erase Shivley's pain, if even for a moment, and her heart soared with joy. Too soon Shivley shuddered and collapsed against her, holding her tight. Warm breath filled her mouth as Shivley slowly regained control. Hands that had clenched her cheeks when Shivley climaxed gently released their grip.

Shivley's head was spinning. The temperature of the water along with the heat of their bodies was making her light-headed. Of course, the fact that she had a mind-blowing orgasm in the arms of a beautiful woman probably had something to do with it as well. She found the strength to lift her head and peer into Rachel's eyes.

"I guess I wasn't as tired as I thought I was." She was rewarded with a soft smile.

"That was *not* my intention." *But I sure am glad it worked out this way.*

"Nor mine. But I can't say I'm not pleased with the result." Shivley bent her head and gently kissed the lips she'd ravished only moments earlier.

"We're losing the hot water." Rachel didn't want the moment to end, but she despised tepid water regardless of the circumstances, and that included being naked in the arms of a desirable woman. Shivley reached around her, shut off the water, and lifted her into her arms. Rachel tightened her grip, and she floated in Shivley's arms as she walked across the room.

Shivley needed Rachel's skin next to hers. She needed to feel the warmth of her arms and the comfort of her embrace. Her body craved Rachel's touch. Rachel grounded her, and when she laid Rachel on the bed and covered her body with her own, Shivley felt as if she had finally come home.

CHAPTER TWENTY-FIVE

The sun was not yet above the horizon when Rachel woke. It took a moment for her to realize that she was not in her own bed and she was definitely not alone. Her body flushed at the memory of the many times she and Shivley had made love in the short night. Their coupling mirrored their passion, simmering just below the surface or quickly exploding in a barrage of sensations that consumed Rachel to the point where several times she was not certain she had remained conscious.

Rachel lay quietly so as not to disturb Shivley sleeping beside her. Shivley's brow was furrowed in her sleep and Rachel's hand trembled when she reached out to stroke the tightness. At the first light touch, Shivley stirred and then settled back into sleep. Rachel's pulse beat stronger with every stroke across the soft skin, and something tugged at her heart. She felt a wave of tenderness wash over her that she could very easily allow herself to drown in.

Rachel studied Shivley while she slept. The women Rachel knew didn't have calloused hands and sun-weathered tanned skin. Their boots had four-inch heels and pointed toes, not flat, worn heels caked with dirt. Their hair was always perfect, not like the rumpled curls sharing her pillow. They were thin almost to the point of unhealthy due to starvation, not firm and lean due to hard work. They smelled like Chanel or Calvin Klein, not sweat, leather, and cattle. Shivley McCoy was definitely not the kind of woman Rachel dated. She scowled. She didn't date. She had sex, and more often than she probably cared to admit, she fucked. Her love life was as impersonal and transitory as the rest of her life.

Rachel shuddered when she realized what had been missing in her relationships. She didn't know any better, and as a result hadn't really thought about it. She was content and happy with the way things were. She intended to never put herself in a position where she could get hurt, and for that she got an A+, but it was a very hollow accomplishment. The phrase "you don't know what you're missing" came to mind. And at that moment, lying in bed with a cowgirl, Rachel admitted, was where she wanted to be for the rest of her life.

Stunned at her admission, Rachel stared at the face inches from hers. She knew lust and desire and passion for a woman, but she had never *wanted* one. Ever since Shivley almost ran into her on the road, Rachel had yearned for her attention, her touch, and the safety of her arms. She didn't know what she was going to do when it was time to leave. She didn't know how Shivley felt about her and realized that when she left, it would not be the same casual "thanks-for-the-good-time-good-bye" that she had mastered years ago. She didn't want to think what that meant.

When Rachel woke several hours later she was alone. She touched the bed where Shivley had lain and it was cold, indicating she'd been up for some time. Rachel momentarily felt a pang of regret that Shivley didn't wake her, but quickly remembered the incident last night and suspected she had things to attend to. She tossed off the covers eager to see Shivley. Just being with her was enough.

❖

"Come on, Shivley, what's the real story? You look like shit."

Shivley was sitting at the kitchen table nursing a cup of coffee when Ann had walked in. Obviously Ann didn't believe her when she told her nothing was wrong. She recapped the events of the previous night in detail, omitting the parts where she and Rachel made love. "Jesus, Ann, I had no idea," Shivley continued but was quickly interrupted.

"Shivley, it's all right. It's what Dale would have wanted you to do. If she were alive today she'd give you holy hell for agonizing over this. She loved you too much to see you like this."

Shivley ran her hands though her damp hair. The events of last night had come flooding back at her when she was in the shower, and she was still shaken by it. "No, Ann, that's not it."

Ann sat down beside her and covered her hand with her own. "Then what is it, Shivley?"

"Dale and I were through a long time before she died. But I didn't have the guts to do anything about it. I just kept going. And then she got sick. I loved her, Ann, I really did, but I wasn't in love with her. I couldn't even get it together to love her when she was dying." Shivley sipped at the lukewarm coffee. "And then she died. I felt so guilty for not loving her enough to try harder, to make it work. To make her last days and months truly happy, knowing that I loved her."

"She knew you loved her," Ann said softly.

"Not like she deserved. She deserved someone who

worshipped the ground she walked on. Someone who thought she was brighter than any star in the sky. Someone who would do anything for her. That wasn't me. It hadn't been for a long time." Shivley dropped her head in her hands, tears spilling onto the table. "She deserved better than me."

"Shivley, you can't eat yourself up over this. You were there when it mattered. You. No one else. Christ, her parents weren't even decent enough to be there. You were there because you wanted to be, not because you had to be. There's a difference."

"I know that, Ann, and I want to put it behind me but…it's just that…" She trailed off, uncertain of what she would say next.

"It's what?" Ann asked encouragingly.

"I'm happier now than I ever was with Dale. It took her dying for me to have all of this. A wonderful woman, a great friend, a fabulous teacher had to die so I could be happy. How terrible is that? I don't deserve this. I don't deserve to be living this life and loving Ra—" She stopped before she said any more.

"Shivley, what are you talking about? Of course you deserve this, to be happy. Where did you ever get that idea?" Ann sat back in her chair, realization dawning on her face. "Is that why you haven't… Shivley, is that why you haven't been with anyone?"

"Ann, it's more complicated than that." At least from her vantage point it was.

"Really? How so?"

The more time that passed after Dale's death, the more Shivley had begun to see more clearly exactly what their relationship had become. She was not in love with Dale when she died. Yes, she loved her, but as she would a close friend, not as a lover. Their relationship had faded and she hadn't even realized it. She had mourned for Dale but not as she would have if she were desperately in love with her. Out of the haze of sadness, Shivley had begun to feel like a hypocrite or worse—a prostitute. She had collected Dale's life insurance and inherited her estate as if she deserved it. And she wasn't sure she did. It was only because Dale had died she was in the position she was in right now.

Her voice cracked when she said she wasn't in love with Dale the way everyone thought she was. She lowered her eyes when she talked about the outpouring of sympathy she had received when Dale had died and how she didn't deserve any of it. She told her that she felt guilty for dragging Ann out here to take care of her under the false impression that she was falling apart. At that point Ann cut her off.

"Shivley." When she didn't look at her, Ann repeated her name, this time more sternly. "Shivley, look at me. Don't be so hard on yourself. You deserve every bit of sympathy and caring you received. We are your friends, always have been. Always will be. You and Dale were together for four years and just because the love you shared was no longer the searing passion it once was doesn't mean you didn't suffer a huge loss."

"What kind of person am I that I get to have everything I want? Dale wanted a life with me and she died thinking she had it. But she didn't. I didn't love her. The woman was dying and I didn't love her. I shortchanged a dying woman out of everything she wanted. And what do I do? I buy this ranch and live happily ever after. And you know what else? I slept with Rachel." Ann's face showed her surprise. "Yeah, not once or twice. We made love at least a dozen times. I never should have let it happen. It never should have happened." Shivley accentuated every word separately. "I cannot do this."

Rachel didn't hang around to hear any more. She had finished her shower and bounded down the stairs in search of Shivley filled with a joy for the new day. She had not felt this good in a long, long time. When she heard voices in the kitchen she stopped, not wanting to interrupt, but when Shivley mentioned her involvement last night she couldn't help but listen. Her heart clenched at the words she heard coming from the woman who had held her so gently the night before. A wave of nausea rushed over her, and Rachel reached out and grabbed the wall for support. She had eavesdropped long enough.

❖

"How could I be so stupid?" Rachel was tightening the cinch on Bonanza's saddle and didn't expect an answer from the big gelding. In one practiced, swift motion she was in the saddle and nudging her horse out the door. She stopped long enough to tell Bart where she was going and spurred Bonanza to the north.

The sun was high in the sky when Rachel finally stopped. She was so distracted by Shivley's words echoing in her brain she paid little attention to sore muscles overworked from the night before. She carefully sat down on the ground on the opposite side of a tree where she tethered the horse. Taking her hat off, she leaned back, vaguely noticing the rough surface of the tree as it poked her back. The pain numbed any further discomfort, and she ran her hands through her damp hair.

"What an idiot." At her loud tone of voice, Bonanza glanced up from nibbling on wild grass. "I can't believe I allowed myself to fall for her. What in the fuck was I thinking? Jesus, Rachel, she even named this ranch after her dead lover." The only answer to Rachel's question came from the birds chirping overhead. "You're right. I wasn't thinking, not at all. And look where it got me. I know better. People are always out for something or have something to hide. I guess with Shivley I got both."

She repeated the question in her head that she had asked again. "How could I be so stupid?" An overwhelming sadness blanketed her like a wet cloth. Shivley wasn't interested in anything other than living with the guilt of her dead lover. She was still hung up on Dale, and guilt was one thing Rachel wanted nothing to do with. Rachel had fallen in love with Shivley and now she had to get over it and get back on track with her life.

Rachel plucked several blades of grass and let them fall between her fingers one by one. She stopped when the childhood chant "She loves me, she loves me not" came to mind. Her tears mixed with the remaining grass she dropped to the ground.

❖

Rachel returned just as the dinner bell rang. She barely said a word to Shivley, who had begun to worry when she had not returned by early afternoon. She was getting ready to saddle her horse and go look for her when Rachel rode into the stable. Shivley followed Rachel inside.

"I was worried about you." *Worried, hell, I was scared to death.*

Rachel knew Shivley was behind her but didn't turn around. "Bart knew where I was."

"Yes, he told me you went riding, but I was still worried." Shivley wanted to put her arms around Rachel, relieved that she'd come back unharmed, but Rachel's aloofness stopped her.

"You don't have to worry about me, Shivley. I'm perfectly capable of taking care of myself." Rachel's voice bit with sarcasm.

"I don't doubt that, but I was worried just the same." Shivley had no idea what the problem was.

Rachel shrugged, her back still to her. She heaved the heavy saddle onto the stand. "That's right, I'm a paying customer and I suppose you have to be worried about liability and shit like that."

The bitterness in Rachel's words propelled Shivley forward. She put her hand on Rachel's shoulder to turn her around, but Rachel beat her to it.

"Don't touch me."

Shivley's heart skipped, the anger in Rachel's eyes stunning her. "What's the matter? What's going on, Rachel?" She was not expecting this type of reaction. Not twelve hours earlier she'd woken in the arms of this beautiful woman who had comforted her without question. They had lain together, talking quietly, gently making love over and over again.

"I said don't touch me." Rachel said the words, but her gut clenched at every one of them. The look of hurt and confusion on Shivley's face was almost her undoing.

Shivley stepped back, her hands in front of her, palms out in surrender. "Okay, okay. Jeez, take it easy. I wasn't going to hurt you."

"You're too late."

Rachel started to storm past, but Shivley couldn't let her go without getting to the bottom of this inane conversation. She stepped in front of Rachel, blocking her exit. She searched Rachel's eyes, looking for the answer to her questions. "What are you talking about? Too late for what?"

Rachel shook her head in disbelief. "You figure it out."

Shivley watched Rachel walk away, bewildered by the harsh words. She had no idea what might have happened that caused Rachel to react like this. On the contrary, Shivley was hoping that they could spend some quiet time together tonight without all the drama of the night before. It certainly didn't appear to be the way the evening was shaping up.

The women surrounding the oval table were in a talkative mood, having rested most of the day, either in their rooms or on the porch. Several conversations were going on simultaneously involving everyone except Rachel, who sat quietly at the end of the table. Shivley noticed that she hadn't eaten much dinner but moved the food around her plate to appear as if she had. Rachel's head jerked up at the sound of a name.

"Who?"

"James Crafter, the bastard from South Dakota. Who does he think he is, trying to control a woman's body like that?" Christina asked the question.

Shivley had one ear listening to the conversation at the other end of the table. The women were talking about the senator from South Dakota who'd cast the deciding vote on a bill that would require a forty-eight-hour waiting period to get an abortion after a woman had seen a doctor. It was a controversial subject in and of itself, but put it in a room full of lesbians and three bottles of wine, and you had a passionate discussion.

"He's a good guy," Rachel replied without thinking.

"Are you nuts?" Jane countered. "He's a... Wait a minute. Did you get him reelected?"

The turn in the conversation was all too familiar to Rachel. She didn't answer.

"How could you do that? Do you know how demeaning it is that some balding, fat white guy is going to force you to wait before you can do something to your own body? That's ridiculous."

Debra piled on. "He has no right, and I can't believe any self-respecting lesbian would have anything to do with him, let alone help him get reelected."

There was no doubt as to what they thought of her now. Rachel was not in the mood to argue. Crafter was a staunch supporter of children and education, homeless shelters, and drug rehabs. He had an excellent plan to overhaul the state foster care system and had discussed it with Rachel several times. Rachel had closed an eye to one thing, believing that the others made up for it several times over.

When Jackie and Ellen started in on Rachel, Shivley finally spoke up. Rachel had not answered the question, but everyone in the room knew the answer. She, too, was appalled that Rachel could work for a man who thought that way, but she didn't voice her opinion. "Ladies, please. Rachel is a guest here and as such I insist on respecting her. Let's just agree to disagree and talk about something else, shall we?" Shivley looked at Rachel, who wore a mask of indifference across her face. Eyes that previously sparkled were now flat and dark.

Rachel excused herself from the table and went to her room. She filled the tub, and as she was about to step into the steamy water, there was a knock on the door. She knew who it was and debated with herself if she should answer it or not. Before she had a chance to decide, Shivley called her name.

"Rachel? Rachel, I know you're in there. Please open the door." Shivley leaned close to the door and listened. She didn't hear any movement inside, but she knew Rachel was behind the locked door. She put her forehead on the cool door. "Rachel, please open the door."

After her conversation with Ann that morning she had thought of nothing other than Rachel all day. She remembered the rest of their conversation. *"You know what the kicker is, Ann? I'm happier than I ever could be with Dale, either with or without this ranch. Rachel is everything Dale wasn't. She loves the ranch. She's a natural here. It feels right when she rides next to me. We work well together. She seems to know exactly what I want even before I know it. The world is a better place with Rachel by my side. But I don't deserve her, and she deserves someone better than me."*

The oak door muffled Shivley's voice, but Rachel could clearly hear that she was almost pleading. She knew she couldn't stay locked in her room for two days. Well, she could, but that would be the chicken's way out, and Rachel was anything but. When faced with a problem or an ugly situation, she prided herself on tackling it head-on. Why should this be any exception? Wrapping her robe tightly around herself, she walked silently across the room. The floor was cool on her bare feet and she shivered slightly as she approached the door. She took a deep, steadying breath and turned the knob.

Shivley had just about given up any hope that Rachel would talk to her and almost fell into the room when she opened the door. Rachel stood before her in the terry-cloth robe, dark circles around her eyes. It felt like someone was reaching in, grabbing her heart, and ripping it out to see Rachel like this. She wanted so badly to talk to Rachel, had thought of nothing other than that all day, and now that she had the opportunity, Shivley's mind went blank.

"May I come in?"

Rachel looked at her as if trying to decide to let her in or slam the door in her face. Shivley breathed a sigh of relief when she stepped back and the door fell open. She took four or five steps into the room. She turned around when she heard the door close. Rachel was standing with her back to the door, her hands buried deep in the pockets of the robe.

"Rachel, what's wrong? Don't tell me nothing because we both know better. What happened between last night and this morning?" Shivley had no idea. It didn't look like Rachel was going to answer her. "Rachel?"

"Nothing happened, Shivley. Last night was great, but

that was all it was. Like I said earlier in the week, I needed a good fuck and you were kind enough to oblige."

Shivley was shocked. That was the last thing she expected to hear. "Kind enough to oblige? Jesus Christ, Rachel, you make it sound like I did you a favor."

"You didn't let me finish. I was going to say and you needed it as much as I did. We came together at the right time and it was great, but that's it. It happened, nothing more, nothing less." It took all of Rachel's skill to maintain her composure. She had been hurt enough. She of all people had no idea how to have a normal relationship, whatever that was, and the ghost of Dale hovering over them would make it impossible. She refused to be the fool. Emotional distance was what she was good at, and she reached down and pulled it out now. She was going to come out ahead like she always had in every other relationship that had gone sour.

Rachel's coolness surprised Shivley. She looked hard into Rachel's eyes, searching for a chink in the armor she had effectively pulled on. She stared for what seemed like an eternity, but Rachel did not back down.

"If that's the way you want it. But it's bullshit, Rachel, and I know it. It meant something to me and it meant something to you. I understand what you're doing, and if this is what you have to do, then I can't do anything other than respect it. But it's a load of crap." Shivley played a hunch in believing that what they had shared the night before was more than just two women fulfilling a need. No one made love as tenderly as Rachel had made love to her and thought it meant nothing.

Rachel wanted to lose herself in Shivley's arms again, but she wouldn't be second fiddle, especially to the memories of a dead woman. From what she'd heard this morning, Shivley regretted what had happened between them, and that was all that needed to be said.

"Is that all?" Rachel's voice was flat, emotionless, and didn't encourage any further conversation. Shivley wanted to fight for her and Rachel, but she didn't deserve anyone, especially a woman as wonderful as Rachel. She didn't answer, but walked past Rachel and out the bedroom door.

CHAPTER TWENTY-SIX

The remaining two days were the longest of Shivley's life. She had to give Rachel credit. She had not avoided her or any of the other guests and had participated in all the scheduled activities. Gone were the enthusiasm and intuitiveness, and her heart was definitely not in it. Meals were awkward, with Rachel avoiding eye contact with her while joining in the conversations.

The evening before the women were scheduled to leave Shivley watched as Rachel went out the front door. Shivley heard her boots cross the porch and knew she was headed toward the stables. She followed a few minutes later. Rachel was saying good-bye to Bonanza, and Shivley stepped behind a large pillar to allow Rachel her privacy. She gently stroked the big gelding's head, her hands running up and down his nose and around his ears. She was whispering something in his ears that calmed the animal, and with one last look over her shoulder, she walked away.

Shivley almost stepped out of her hiding place, but didn't. There was nothing to say to Rachel. Nothing that would change the way things were or the way she felt toward her. She loved

Rachel but knew there was no way anything good could ever come from it. She let her pass. Rachel turned off the light and Shivley stood alone in the dark for a very long time.

❖

Almost everyone was on board. One by one the women had said their good-byes and boarded the plane that would take them back to their normal lives. Rachel was the last to board, and picking up her duffel, she stopped in front of Shivley. She had not slept a wink last night knowing she would never see Shivley McCoy again. She tried to convince herself that this was just a vacation and nothing more, but after several hours she simply gave in to thinking about the last nine days.

Nothing in her life had ever come as close to pure happiness as her time at the ranch. She'd been one person when she arrived and was a very different person now that she was leaving. She had found herself again at the Springdale and was not going to let it disappear again. But the ranch was only part of it. Shivley was the rest. She was the one Rachel had risked everything for, and it had bounced back in her face. Rachel had been so sure about Shivley—she was still trying to figure out where she had misread her.

"Good-bye, Rachel."

Shivley's voice was calm, but Rachel saw that her eyes were sad. *Ask me to stay. Please tell me I'm the one who can make you forget about Dale. Please ask me to stay.* "Good-bye, Shivley." The other women had either shaken hands with Shivley or given her a quick hug. Rachel couldn't bear to do either. A handshake was ludicrous, and if she put her arms around Shivley again, she might never let go. Rachel did neither. She turned and climbed the same seven steps that changed her life ten days ago.

❖

Shivley waved a final good-bye to her guests. She loved giving women the opportunity to experience a snippet of life on a ranch, but she was never so happy to see a bunch of women leave in her life. She had almost managed to evade the clutches of Christina, but she was so preoccupied with thoughts of Rachel, she didn't see Christina until it was too late. By then Christina had her arms around her neck and had her locked in a sloppy kiss. Shivley pried her off an instant before Christina's tongue would have been down her throat.

Shivley turned her back on the plane and climbed into her Jeep. She was edgy and at a loss as to what to do next. There were dozens of things that needed tending to- –there were fences to repair, stock to check on, and grass to mow—but as Shivley sat in her Jeep, all she could do was relive the moment she'd first laid eyes on Rachel Stanton.

She hadn't realized it then, but looking back on it now, Shivley saw with clarity just how much Rachel had affected her. Yes, she was immediately attracted to her, who wouldn't be? She was absolutely beautiful, but it was something else. Shivley knew what it was. She had fallen in love with Rachel, plain and simple. Her spirit soared every time Rachel said her name. Her heart pounded in her chest when she watched Rachel on her horse or in the barn, and when she touched her, well, that was more than she could ever imagine.

Rachel's touch was like fire. She knew just what to do and did it extremely well. She could sense when Shivley needed more pressure or a feather-light touch. Rachel made her quiver on the edge of desire just long enough before taking her over that edge. Shivley felt strong and powerful and sensual in Rachel's arms. Rachel brought joy and happiness back into her life in just a few days. But it wasn't that simple. They lived in two worlds that could not be more different.

Shivley's musings were interrupted when Ann slipped into the seat beside her. "Wanna talk about it?"

"No."

"Too bad, talk to me about it anyway."

Shivley shook her head in disbelief. "You know, Ann, if you ever decide to leave here, you could make a killing as a psychic."

"Yes, I could, but I'm not leaving, and don't try to change the subject," Ann replied sternly.

"I'm in love with her." Shivley didn't think she would ever say those three words again.

"Does she know that?"

"No." Shivley's voice cracked.

"Why not?"

"I didn't tell her."

"Why not?"

"I'll never be able to give her what she needs." *Or what she deserves*, Shivley thought.

"And what does she need other than your love?"

Shivley exhaled deeply and gazed out the windshield. Thunderclouds that mirrored her disposition darkened the sky, threatening to rain at any moment. Shivley was afraid that when the sky opened up she would, too. "Rachel had a difficult childhood. She never said it exactly, but I don't think she trusts many people, or anyone for that matter." Shivley continued to tell Ann what she knew about Rachel's life. "She's been disappointed too many times in her life, and I can't add to that."

"Why do you think you would?"

A drop of rain hit the windshield of the Jeep, then another, and another. "Because I'm afraid that I wouldn't be able to love her the way she needs to be loved, the way she deserves to be loved." That was Shivley's biggest fear. She loved Rachel too much to disappoint her or cause her any pain. "I'm afraid we'll end up like Dale, and I can't do that to her."

"So you're not going to do anything?"

"That's right." Clouds rumbled in the distance.

Ann turned to her. "So let me get this straight. You love Rachel and she loves you." Ann stopped when Shivley turned to look at her. "Come on, Shivley. I saw the way she looked at you. She couldn't take her eyes off you when you were in the room. And when you weren't, she was like a caged lion looking for you. She might not be ready to admit it, but she does. What is with you women these days?"

"Ann," Shivley began.

"No, don't Ann me. You're going to be too pigheaded to go after her because you think you *might* end up like you and Dale? Shivley, you have a better chance of winning the lottery than what you're afraid of. You know why?"

"I'm sure you're going to tell me."

"You're goddamned right I am." Ann was angry now. "Because *this* you can control. *You can control it. If you really want to.*" The rain on the soft top of the Jeep sounded like the tapping of sticks. "So what are you going to do about it?"

Shivley turned the key in the ignition. "Nothing." She shifted the Jeep into gear. Ann reached over and put a hand on her arm. Shivley cut her off before Ann even had a chance to begin. "Ann, it's pointless. She has a high-powered job and lives in Atlanta. For Christ's sake, she'll probably be responsible for the next president! I'm just a simple cowpoke living in the boondocks with cows and horses."

"I seem to remember Rachel kicking ass on her horse. She also knew exactly what to do the night of the storm. She was the only one out of all those women who had even the slightest idea of what it takes to run this ranch. Don't tell me she couldn't be happy here. And don't tell yourself that either." Ann crossed her arms over her chest.

"I won't ask her to leave her life. For what? For this?" Shivley's hands were palms up, indicating all that lay in front of them. "To work your hands to the bone and be so tired you can't even stay awake long enough to eat? To castrate cattle, shovel shit, and shoot horses when they get injured? To be so hot you'd think you'd die of sunstroke and so cold you're afraid you won't?" Shivley's voice had risen and she wasn't sure who she was trying to convince, Ann or herself.

"No. For you."

Ann's voice was soft, but the words echoed through Shivley's brain like a freight train.

❖

Rachel dropped her duffel bag in the foyer and headed straight for the shower. Her flight, though relatively short, was miserable, her mind jumping back and forth between life with Shivley and life without. The red light was blinking on her answering machine when she got out of the shower, but Rachel chose to ignore it and headed straight for bed. She fell asleep as soon as her head hit the pillow.

The next morning she had breakfast at the local coffee shop and stopped at the store to restock her refrigerator. After putting the perishables in the fridge, she grabbed a cold beer and headed out to the deck. The phone rang as she opened the sliding door and she debated whether or not to answer it. She was not in the mood to talk to anyone and certainly did not want to talk to anyone from the office.

Four beers later Rachel was still on edge. She had flipped through the channels, tried to read a book, and even gone for a walk, but nothing could shake the awkward feeling she would describe as out of sorts. It made no sense to her. She was back home, in her element, where she was in control and knew every move she was going to make and the next two moves of her opponent. She should feel secure, but what she felt was unsettled. In the past she would have attributed it to being away from the office for so long. She would simply get back into her routine and she would be fine. But this time, Rachel wasn't so sure she would get over it.

The sun was setting behind the trees when she finally went inside. She puttered around in the kitchen, and on the way to the laundry room to start a load of clothes, she pushed the Play button on the answering machine.

The first message was from Senator Denton upping the ante, hoping to convince Rachel to join his campaign. Rachel was surprised when the familiar tickle of interest went up her neck. The insane compensation he quoted was enough to take it seriously. Prior to going to Springdale, she had been sick of the political scene, the backstabbing, and the deals that required you to sell your little sister in order to get your bill passed later. She had little interest in the thrill of the chase, and definitely not the slimeballs that accompanied it.

But what was she going to do the rest of her life? Fortunately she had been paid well and invested even better, and had enough money in the bank that she didn't need to worry about it for quite some time. Perhaps she'd take a trip to Europe or maybe Australia. All of these thoughts went through her mind while the senator from the great state of New Hampshire droned on. She hit the Erase button and he finally stopped. She picked up the phone.

❖

The woman staring back at her in the mirror was a stranger. Rachel was in another hotel room in yet another city, and she had no idea who she was looking at. *Who is this woman?* She was wearing an impeccably tailored Armani business suit, silk stockings, and a pair of eight-hundred-dollar Prada shoes. Her nails were buffed to a blazing shine, and two-carat diamond earrings winked at her. The three-hundred-dollar haircut was perfect for her face and had just a hint of highlights. Rachel had seen a string of strangers in this similar position, but none that looked exactly like her.

Again she asked, this time out loud, "Who in the hell are you?"

Rachel had been back to work for a month directing the campaign of the man most whispered to be the next presidential candidate. She had named her price—huge, her role in the campaign—strategic, and her travel accommodations—first class and five star. They were met without hesitation and here she was, in a hotel room with a total stranger—herself.

Rachel didn't recognize herself anymore. Yes, the clothes, hotels, limos, and private planes were familiar, but they paled in comparison to jeans, boots, cotton sheets, and horse shit. Where she once thrived on the power, the gamesmanship, and the thrill of victory, she now wanted the simple life of quiet nights in front of the fire watching the stars twinkle. She was a totally different person and she had no idea what to do about it. She didn't even know why she was doing it. Maybe it was because it was familiar, maybe it was mindless work, maybe she didn't have anything else in her life to do?

There was not a minute to spare on the political stump, but Rachel still had too much time alone. In the past she would have occupied herself with a woman, or several women, but she was oddly celibate since returning from her vacation. And it was during those times of solitude that she could not stop thinking about Shivley.

She was more woman than Rachel had ever known and

definitely more than she could handle. She was confident, self-assured, practical, honest, and drop-dead gorgeous. She was clever, funny, spontaneous, and smart. She was everything Rachel could ever want all wrapped up in one. She was magnificent. And she could never love again.

Shivley had said as much to Ann, and as much as Rachel had started to believe she could actually have something with her, a relationship, she couldn't let it happen. What she felt for Shivley had the ability to hurt her, the deep, soul-wrenching kind of hurt that you never really recover from, and Rachel could not let that happen again. She would not let it happen.

CHAPTER TWENTY-SEVEN

Another day, another airport, another flight, but that was where the similarities ended. Rachel was crowded into a twenty-year-old 737 as it taxied down the runway. Billings Airport was small, serving the neighboring communities of rural Montana. Rachel stepped out of the plane and descended the stairs to the tarmac.

She had not checked a bag—she wouldn't be staying long—and she made her way to the car rental counter. Twenty minutes later she was in the driver's seat of a Chevy Tahoe with a cup of coffee in one hand and a map lying on the seat beside her. Before she pulled out of the parking lot she checked the map for directions. Smiling, she remembered another time when she checked a map for directions.

The roads were mostly empty, and although there were dark clouds on the horizon, the August sun was shining brightly, creating a glare that was unbearable without her sunglasses. As she turned left at the intersection of Route 33 and Barkley Road, the memories flooded her consciousness like a tidal wave. The fence was the same barbed wire she had helped put up over twenty years ago. The flag was up on the mailbox at the end of the drive. The tires of the Tahoe cracked over the crushed granite as she pulled in and parked next to an old Chevy pick-up truck. She turned off the engine and sat staring at the house.

The Stewarts had recently painted it a soft shade of brown with chocolate trim around the doors and windows. On the front porch stood three rocking chairs, three empty flower containers, and a door mat. Rachel immediately thought of the doormat that was there when she was. Welcome. She hadn't felt welcome when she arrived then, but she did now. She steeled herself and stepped out of the truck.

It had taken very little to track down the Stewarts. Actually, all it took was a phone call to directory assistance and she was talking to them on the phone. Susan and Raymond still lived in the same house and were still foster parents for children in the area.

She had called the Stewarts because her life was in turmoil. She didn't know what she wanted to do. She had tried the easy answer, but after only a few days she knew the political trail was no longer for her. She couldn't sleep, she had lost weight, and she barked at everybody.

Her hand trembled as she knocked on the door. Several seconds passed and she thought maybe she should turn around and go back to Atlanta. Before she had a chance to make a decision, the front door opened. The smiling face and warm eyes in front of her told her she had made the right decision. She'd had the idea to visit the Stewarts when she was thinking about a certain tall, lanky rancher. The connection was clear, and she was on the phone in an instant.

"Rachel?" Susan Stewart asked tentatively.

Rachel nodded. "Miss Susan, it's good to see you again." Rachel was immediately engulfed in an enormous hug. Tears sprang up and threatened to overflow onto the shoulder of one of her many foster mothers.

"Come on inside." Rachel was unceremoniously led into the house. The living room had different furniture and drapes, but was just as she remembered. The smell brought her back to the first day she stepped inside this house, and she could have sworn she was thirteen again. And just as scared.

"Raymond, she's here. Rachel is here," Susan yelled in the direction of the kitchen. "Let me take your coat."

Rachel passed her coat to Mrs. Stewart just as a man at least six inches shorter than she was walked into the room. He stopped and looked at her head to toe. He broke out in a wide grin.

"Mr. Raymond, how are you, sir?" Rachel asked politely. When she had first come here to this house the Stewarts told her to call them Miss Susan and Mr. Raymond. Calling them Mr. and Mrs. was too formal, and their first names too disrespectful. They settled on a combination of the two.

"Well, look at you. This can't be the same spunky little girl that always had grease up to her elbows and horse shit on her boots. Rachel, you have turned into a beautiful woman." Raymond Stewart walked over to Rachel and hugged her so tightly she thought he might break a rib. Finally, he released her. "Thank you so much for coming."

They settled in the living room, and Susan served coffee. Rachel had contacted the Stewarts and asked if she could see them. She had an overwhelming need to thank them for putting up with her for three years. They were the only people who had truly made a difference in her life and she wanted them to know. They were thrilled to hear from her and had immediately invited her to come.

The first few minutes were awkward, none of them knowing exactly what to say. They were practically strangers, after all. But after a while they began reminiscing about Rachel's time on their ranch. They asked Rachel what she was doing now and if she had ever married.

"Why did you become foster parents?" Rachel asked. She never understood why people would willingly bring other people's kids into their home. There was always the chance that the kids would be disruptive or worse. It was a risk every foster parent took every time a child was placed in their home.

"We were never to have any children of our own," Susan said, "and we wanted children, lots of them. We read an article in the paper one day about becoming foster parents, and it seemed to fit. If we could not have the children we so desperately wanted, then we would give other children the home they so desperately needed." Raymond reached over and took his wife's hand.

"How many kids did you have?" There were three other kids when she was at the Stewarts.

Susan looked at her husband. "How many have we had, Raymond? Thirty or so?"

"Last count was thirty-two, including Rachel here," he answered.

Thirty-two children. *Jesus*. The unfortunate thing was that at least ten times that many needed a home like the one the Stewarts provided. Suddenly Rachel felt very blessed.

"How did you ever put up with me?"

Susan answered first. "Patience."

"And you were a natural on a horse," Raymond finished. "Have you kept up your riding? You looked so at home on top of a horse."

"Off and on. I was recently at a dude ranch in Arizona for a week or so. It brought back so many memories. I guess it's like riding a bike. You never really forget how, but you sure are sore once you get back on." All three laughed.

"That's why I came back here. I felt so at home at Springdale, that was the name of the ranch there. I drive a fancy car and wear expensive clothes and sleep on silk sheets, and I had no idea I would feel as relaxed and at ease as I did. I was familiar with the routine, remembered how to put a bridle on a stubborn horse and had forgotten the smell of fresh-mown hay." Rachel could smell it even now.

She looked both Stewarts in the eye. "I want to thank you for what you did for me. I don't know where I would be if it wasn't for you. You made a significant impression on my life and I can't thank you enough. I just wanted you to know that." Tears spilled down her cheeks. Susan grabbed a tissue from the box and sat beside her on the couch.

"No need to thank us, Rachel. We loved you the minute we laid eyes on you. We knew you were going to turn out to be somebody special. We only helped with the road markers here and there."

Susan could not have been more wrong, Rachel thought. She and her husband had been the only people that had ever seen more in her than a paycheck. As a wild teenager, Rachel hadn't realized it; she'd seen only the restrictions placed on her by yet another family that was not hers. Her maturity now had cleared her eyes and what she saw brought tears to her eyes. "Miss Susan, you and your husband did more than just help with road markers. You paved the way, and I will be forever grateful."

Susan and Raymond invited Rachel to stay for dinner and they chatted until late in the evening. Thunder rumbled and a heavy rain had begun to fall, and Raymond insisted she spend the night. They put her in her old room and she stepped back in time when she stepped into the room.

Later that evening she and Raymond were sitting in the living room drinking a short tumbler of scotch. Susan had gone to bed a few minutes earlier, claiming an early day tomorrow. The comfortable silence was interrupted by Raymond.

"What's troubling you, Rachel?"

Raymond always had the uncanny knack to see right through her even when she wasn't aware there was anything to see. She told him as much and he laughed. "How did you know Miss Susan was the one for you?" Rachel asked tentatively.

"I took one look at her and fell in love. And the fact that she was fussing at me at the same time didn't bother me one bit. I thought she was the prettiest thing I had ever seen. And spunky, she was all that and more. I knew from the get-go that she would always keep me on my toes and I would never get tired of being with her. It's been forty-eight years, and she has never once let me down."

Rachel longed for the certainly this man had. "Surely you've had disagreements. How do you make it work?"

Raymond laughed. "Disagreements? I'll say. She didn't want nothing to do with me at first."

"What did you do to change her mind?"

"I just kept after her. Kept telling her that I was the one for her and someday she was going to marry me. Pretty soon she realized she had to marry me or I wouldn't shut up."

"How have you kept it together all these years?" Rachel was looking for the magic answer.

"Hard work, lots of talking, tears, and love. When you want something to work, Rachel, you do everything in your power to see that it does. That means no lying, cheating, or taking each other for granted. Don't tell anyone I said this, but I'd be half the man I am today if I didn't have Susan beside me. She makes me want to be a better man for her, a better person. Everything I do I do for her or because of her." Raymond sat back in his chair.

"That sounds like you gave up your life for her. Who you were." This was Rachel's biggest fear.

"I did. My life was nothing until I met Susan. Sure, I had a job, a fast car, and even had some faster women, but it was really nothing. Today I'm a man who makes a difference in the world. Sure, I gave up who I was, but I'd do it again in a heartbeat if given the chance."

"Weren't you afraid?"

Raymond chuckled. "Scared shitless was more like it. But anything worth having is worth fighting for. If you fight hard and lose, you can still look at yourself in the mirror every day. If you don't fight at all…"

Raymond didn't have to finish the sentence. Rachel knew exactly what he was saying. She didn't find it odd that she and Raymond were talking about something as serious and intimate so soon after meeting each other again. Right from the beginning Raymond seemed to understand her like no one else ever had or ever did. Until she met Shivley.

"Have you met someone, Rachel?"

"Yes." Rachel didn't hesitate answering.

"And you're worried if he's the right one?"

"Actually, Mr. Raymond, I'm worried that *she* is the right one."

Rachel was surprised when all Raymond said was, "Tell me about her." They talked until the sun began to peek over the horizon. Raymond kissed her on the cheek at the door to her old bedroom and Rachel fell into bed exhausted.

On her drive to the airport Rachel thought about the love she felt in the Stewart home. She hadn't had much exposure to couples that had a healthy, loving relationship, and she remembered how the Stewarts were with each other. There was honesty and respect and the constant awareness of the other. Rachel finally understood what Shivley was referring to that one night they'd talked by the corral. The Stewarts had it, Shivley had it and wanted it again, and Rachel wanted it for the first time. Twenty quiet minutes later she was standing at the Skywest ticket counter with her American Express card, ready to go home.

CHAPTER TWENTY-EIGHT

"Shivley, what's wrong?" Ann asked.

Shivley had just returned from checking the fence line on the west side of the ranch and had been at it all day. At midafternoon she stopped for water at the stream where she and the last set of guests had had lunch. The place reminded her of Rachel. Hell, everyplace reminded her of Rachel. Ever since she admitted that she had fallen in love with Rachel, she could not get her out of her mind. Rachel was the last thing she thought of before she fell asleep tormented by dreams of her, and the first thing she thought of when she woke up.

Shivley closed her eyes and saw Rachel's smile and heard her laugh. Warmth spread through her when she flashed back to when they worked together side by side keeping the herd calm the night of the big storm. It had felt so good to have a woman at her side again. It had felt good to have Rachel by her side.

"I'm fine, Ann. Just a little tired." Half of it was the truth. She hadn't slept a full night since Rachel left, and that was over two months ago. Another two batches of guests had come and gone, and she was glad for the month-long reprieve until the next group arrived.

"Have you spoken to Rachel?" Ann asked from across the kitchen table. She had just poured them a cup of coffee.

Shivley's head jerked up. Ann's question came out of nowhere and she was not prepared. "No." She pretended to not understand Ann's question. Ann didn't buy it.

"Rachel…"

"Ann, I have nothing to say to her." Shivley tried out her excuse. "And just what exactly would I say?" Shivley knew what she would say, what she dreamed of saying, but knew she never would.

"How about I love you?"

"How about you're crazy?" Shivley said, angry. Ann had been pestering her to contact Rachel. At first it was several times a day until Shivley told her to stop. Now it was only every few days that she would bring Rachel's name into the conversation.

"I suppose you could say something about her being crazy for leaving, but you might want to save that until a little later in the conversation."

"Are you ever going to let this drop?" She didn't need Ann reminding her of her feelings toward Rachel. She faced it every day. Worse yet, she faced it every night.

"Not until you admit what is going on and do something about it," Ann replied, crossing her legs under the table.

"All right, Ann, for crying out loud." Shivley jumped from the chair, anger boiling over. Lucy skidded out from under the table. "I'm in love with her. I want to be with her. I want her to be with me, here on the ranch." Shivley paced the kitchen, running her hands through her hair. "Are you happy now?"

"No."

"No? What in the fuck do I have to do to get you off my back?"

"Go get her."

Shivley stopped pacing and turned to look at her friend. "What?"

"You heard me."

The calmness in Ann's voice and her demeanor was the exact opposite of Shivley's raging emotions. "Just like that? Just walk up to her and tell her that I love her and ask her to change her entire life and move here with me. Is that about it?" Shivley asked, her hands on her hips defiantly.

"Yep, that's about it." Ann nodded

"Ann, you're out of your mind if you think I'm going to do that." Shivley walked by Ann on her way out of the room. Ann caught her by the arm.

"No, Shivley. You're out of your mind if you don't."

❖

Ann's words were still echoing in her brain when Shivley opened the front door fully intending to escape to the stables. She was startled that someone was standing on the threshold. Shivley's knees grew weak when she recognized Rachel looking impossibly beautiful in the warm glow cast by the porch light.

"Hello, Shivley."

Rachel's voice was soft and sensuous and sounded like a million violins to her ears. Shivley could not believe that Rachel was here, at her house. Why was she here? What could she want? It couldn't be that she… Shivley let the thought drift away. It was too much to hope for.

"Rachel?" Her throat was tight.

"How have you been?" Rachel could not take her eyes off

Shivley. She had been driving for hours thinking about this moment, and almost lost her nerve when the rental car entered the drive.

"I'm well." Shivley couldn't believe she was having such a ridiculous conversation with an ex-lover who lived hundreds of miles away and just happened to show up on her doorstep. "What are you doing here?"

Rachel shifted her weight from foot to foot. "I came to talk to you. To see you." She didn't know exactly what she was going to say when she stepped inside, but she hoped it would be enough.

Shivley shook herself out of her shock. "Oh, sorry, come in." She opened the door wider, and the scent of Rachel floated in the air as she walked by. She smelled just as good as Shivley remembered, and she was taken back to the first time they'd made love in the barn.

"Shivley, don't you run out on me when I'm—" Ann stopped scolding her when she saw Rachel standing in the foyer. "Rachel?"

"Hello, Ann." The look on Ann's face was similar to the one on Shivley's, a combination of shock, disbelief, confusion, happiness, and fear. Ann, however, recovered, whereas Shivley was still stunned.

"It's good to see you, Rachel. I hope you'll be staying for dinner." Ann looked at Shivley when she said it.

"Thank you, Ann. It's good to see you, too." Ann silently left the room and Rachel turned back to Shivley. Shivley didn't say anything but indicated for her to sit.

Rachel sat on the couch, Shivley mercifully sitting beside her. "Is Ann fussing at you again?" Rachel asked tentatively, teasing her.

"Yeah. Seems as though that's her second calling lately." Shivley shrugged.

"It's because she cares about you, you know." Rachel wanted to say that Ann wasn't the only one who cared about her, but something stopped her.

"Yeah, well, this time she means it," Shivley said. Rachel showing up after her argument with Ann had definitely thrown her for a loop. Images of Rachel flashed through her brain like a kaleidoscope. Rachel was everywhere. In her house, on her horses, repairing fences, mucking stalls, riding by her side, and in her bed. Rachel was in all the places Shivley wanted her to be. Where she needed her to be. And she was sitting next to her right now.

Shivley finally took a long look at the woman who had haunted her dreams. Rachel was a little thinner than she remembered and her hair was a little lighter. Her fingernails were manicured and a wide band of silver adorned the ring finger of her right hand. Her jeans were new and she had traded her boots for a pair of well-worn Doc Martens. The sleeves of her blue Henley shirt were pushed up exposing strong, tanned forearms.

"You look tired," Rachel said. She cupped Shivley's cheek, running her thumb lightly across the dark circles under Shivley's eyes. Her heart hurt at the sight.

Shivley couldn't speak. Rachel's soft palm on her face and her fingers in her hair took her breath away. "I've slept better."

At the first touch of Shivley's skin, Rachel almost came unglued. Her skin was warm, almost hot, and her fingers burned. She wanted to touch every inch of Shivley's skin. She needed to touch her, to make sure she was really here and not another of her dreams. "What's keeping you awake?"

Shivley's head cleared a little more each passing minute. She dared to think about why Rachel was sitting in her living room. This wasn't a business meeting. Shivley smiled, her heart beating just a bit faster from the concern she heard in Rachel's voice. "Just the usual stuff in the life of a rancher." She tried to keep it light.

"Tell me about it. I want to know everything there is to know about the life of a certain devilishly attractive, dark-haired rancher," Rachel said, encouraging Shivley to continue. She loved the sound of Shivley's voice, the way she phrased things, and especially the look on her face when she talked about the ranch.

Shivley took a deep breath. The sparkle of interest she saw in Rachel's eyes gave her the encouragement she needed to jump off the cliff she had been standing on ever since Rachel left. "It's lonely," she said simply.

Rachel laughed nervously. "How can it be lonely? The place is crawling with lesbians." And that was her biggest fear, she realized. That Shivley would want someone else.

For the first time since she opened the door, Shivley met her gaze and held it. What she saw gave Rachel hope and encouragement, and it cleared up any remaining doubt as to why she had traveled hundreds of miles to be sitting next to the most beautiful woman she had ever known.

"Because there's no one to share it with," Shivley said without hesitation.

This was the opening Rachel was waiting for. "If you could have anyone in the world to share it with, who would it be? Wait, don't answer that," Rachel said suddenly. She had to do this. She had to take control of her life, and if she was ever going to take a chance on love, to be able to look herself in the mirror, she had to make this move. She had to risk it all.

She took Shivley's hand. "I want to share it with you." Rachel could almost hear her heart opening to this wonderful woman. She had come here to be with Shivley. In that instant Rachel realized just how much she was in love with Shivley.

It had happened so easily, so naturally she had not recognized it, had not seen it coming. Like a thief in the night, the rancher had stolen her heart. Her emotions soared, but she was still afraid it would all come crashing to the ground.

Rachel's eyes never left Shivley's. She had never felt so strong or so frightened. She wanted this, desperately wanted this, and she was not going to let it slip through her fingers again. Everything was at risk here, and Rachel was willingly putting it all out on the table. "I want to be here with you." Rachel caressed Shivley's cheek. "You were right, that night when we made love, it did mean something to me. It meant everything to me. You mean everything to me." The flash in Shivley's eyes boosted her courage.

"I heard you and Ann talking in the kitchen that morning after." Rachel stuttered on the last few words. "You said you regretted making love to me. Well, as much as I run the risk of being hurt, I don't. Regardless of whether or not you want me in your life, I don't regret it at all. You are the best thing that ever happened to me." Rachel finally felt herself relaxing. "I love you, Shivley. I never thought I'd be capable of loving someone, but I do. You have given me another lease on life. I thought I was happy staying just on the edge of feeling anything, but now I see I was a coward. I don't want to be in that safe place anymore because it's too lonely there. There is no one to share it with because it can't be shared. I want to live my life. A life full of emotions. I want to be happy and sad and joyous and so goddamned ecstatic I could shout it from the top of the tallest tree on your beautiful land. What you have here is priceless, Shivley, you are priceless, and I want—no, I hope with all my heart that you want to share it with me. I love you." Rachel took a breath. She felt winded, as if she had just run a marathon.

A thousand thoughts raced through Shivley's mind, one of

which answered the nagging question of what had happened that made Rachel withdraw from her. But the overwhelming realization was that Rachel loved her. This beautiful woman who could have any woman in the world loved her. *Her*, a podunk rancher with a few acres of land and some cattle. Unbelievable. Suddenly the cloud of guilt lifted and she was soaring. But just as suddenly, she thought about Dale. She loved Rachel, and as such, she deserved to know everything.

"I need to tell you something." Shivley watched as Rachel's face dropped. She smiled gently and kissed the palm of her hand.

"I fell for you the minute you stepped out of that ugly rental car. And then when you stepped off the plane, I knew that my life had changed forever. But I was too stupid to realize it at the time. I hid behind some ridiculous sense of propriety about not getting involved with guests when that was exactly what I wanted to do." Rachel looked at their hands, fingers intertwined. Shivley continued.

"I loved Dale. She was a part of my life for a long time, and I can't forget that. I won't forget it. But Dale is in the past. I have come to terms with our relationship and her death. For the longest time I felt guilty for not loving Dale enough. She died not having someone love her like she deserved. She was a warm, wonderful person, and at one time we were happy, I was happy, but in the end, we were just together.

"Sure, I was with her when she got sick and through her treatments because I did love her. I wouldn't have been anywhere else. But I wasn't *in love* with her. I used the money she left me and her life insurance and bought the ranch. It was my dream, not hers, and I used a terrible twist of fate to live my dream." Shivley raised her gaze. "I didn't realize any of this until you came into my life, and even then it took a while for me to figure it out." She chuckled. "Sometimes I'm not the sharpest blade of hay in the stack. It took you leaving and Ann beating some sense into me to realize it."

Rachel had not said a word, so Shivley continued. "I thought I didn't deserve to love someone again. That's because I did such a disservice to Dale that I could never be with anyone else again. I would not do that to someone else. But I now know what Dale and I had, and in the end, what we didn't. It takes two to make a relationship work, and I don't think either one of us had it in us to make it work for us. It wasn't all my fault, and I'm done thinking it was."

Shivley lightly stroked the top of Rachel's soft hands. "It was you I was with when we made love, Rachel, not Dale." Rachel cupped her hand to Shivley's face. "It was always you. And I don't regret a minute of it."

Joy ran rampant in Rachel's heart and threatened to bubble up and explode but was kept at bay by another equally driving emotion: fear. Rachel was afraid of what this meant to her, what this meant for the rest of her life. She had never been able to trust someone enough to have a true relationship. Her heart had been shut down for so long she didn't know what to do or how she should act. But what she did know for certain was that she wanted to learn from Shivley.

"I don't know the first thing about being in a relationship," she said tentatively, almost shyly.

"I'll teach you."

"I'm not used to being around people who truly love each other." Rachel thought about all the political husbands and wives who were together for anything but love.

"You'll be surrounded by them."

Rachel's eyes welled up with tears and she lowered her gaze. She had not cried since her mother left, and it was an unsettling experience. Her voice shook. "I don't know how to trust."

Shivley wiped the tears from Rachel's cheeks and lifted her chin so that she had to look in her eyes. "I will never leave you, Rachel." She had never believed anything more than what she was saying now.

"I don't know how to do this. I'm afraid." It was the first time Rachel had uttered those words.

"I will never leave you, Rachel." Shivley repeated her declaration. "I love you."

Rachel's world started spinning. She wanted to bolt from the room, run away from the panic that was engulfing her like a bad storm. She wanted to crawl back into her safe life where she controlled everything and where fear and uncertainty did not have a place. But she had come here for a reason, and it was to make a life with Shivley. A life built on hope and love and trust. And hard work. Lots of hard work. But the reward was dazzling.

"God, I love you too." Rachel could not remember ever saying those three powerful words. She might have said them to her mother, but she was too young to know what they really meant. She wasn't sure she knew exactly what it meant now, but she was ready to find out.

A slow warming coursed through Shivley's body. She wanted to jump for joy, to run through the street telling everyone she passed that this wonderful woman loved her too. But she knew she would have to take it slow with Rachel. Trust was built on time, and she was going to spend the rest of her life convincing Rachel just how much she loved her.

"Yes, I want to share this with you. There is no one I want by my side except you. There's not much call for a political strategist around here, but you could still do your job. Sky Harbor airport is in Phoenix and not that far away." Shivley wanted Rachel to run the ranch with her. To be beside her every day, but that might not be what Rachel wanted. She was not going to make that mistake twice.

"You asked me once if I was happy shoveling shit all day. I wasn't then, and I certainly won't be in the future. I sold my soul one too many times. I don't know if I chased the money, the challenge, or the glory. One day I didn't like what I saw in the mirror. My life changed when you stepped out of your Jeep and hollered at me." Rachel leaned over and kissed Shivley softly, all her fears sliding away. "I don't want to work anywhere other than right here, with you, every single day." She was rewarded with a smile so bright it was blinding. Shivley stood and grasped her hand.

"Come on, dinner's ready. We've got a big day ahead of us tomorrow."

About the Author

Julie Cannon is a native sun goddess born and raised in Phoenix, Arizona. After a five year stint in "snow up to her #$&" and temperatures that hovered in the 30s, she returned to the Valley of the Sun vowing never to leave again. Julie's day job is in Corporate America and her nights are spent bringing to life the stories that bounce around in her head throughout the day. Julie and her partner Laura have been together for sixteen years and spend their weekends camping, riding ATVs, or lounging around the pool with their seven-year-old son and daughter.

Books Available From Bold Strokes Books

Heartland by Julie Cannon. When political strategist Rachel Stanton and dude ranch owner Shivley McCoy collide on an empty country road, fate intervenes. (978-1-60282-009-8)

Shadow of the Knife by Jane Fletcher. Militia Rookie Ellen Mittal has no idea just how complex and dangerous her life is about to become. A Celaeno series adventure romance. (978-1-60282-008-1)

To Protect and Serve by VK Powell. Lieutenant Alex Troy is caught in the paradox of her life—to hold steadfast to her professional oath or to protect the woman she loves. (978-1-60282-007-4)

Deeper by Ronica Black. Former homicide detective Erin McKenzie and her fiancée Elizabeth Adams couldn't be happier—until the not-so-distant past comes knocking at the door. (978-1-60282-006-7)

The Lonely Hearts Club by Radclyffe. Take three friends, add two ex-lovers and several new ones, and the result is a recipe for explosive rivalries and incendiary romance. (978-1-60282-005-0)

Venus Besieged by Andrews & Austin. Teague Richfield heads for Sedona and the sensual arms of psychic astrologer Callie Rivers for a much-needed romantic reunion. (978-1-60282-004-3)

Branded Ann by Merry Shannon. Pirate Branded Ann raids a merchant vessel to obtain a treasure map and gets more than she bargained for with the widow Violet. (978-1-60282-003-6)

American Goth by JD Glass. Trapped by an unsuspected inheritance and guided only by the guardian who holds the secret to her future, Samantha Cray fights to fulfill her destiny. (978-1-60282-002-9)

Learning Curve by Rachel Spangler. Ashton Clarke is perfectly content with her life until she meets the intriguing Professor Carrie Fletcher, who isn't looking for a relationship with anyone. (978-1-60282-001-2)

Place of Exile by Rose Beecham. Sheriff's detective Jude Devine struggles with ghosts of her past and an ex-lover who still haunts her dreams. (978-1-933110-98-1)

Fully Involved by Erin Dutton. A love that has smoldered for years ignites when two women and one little boy come together in the aftermath of tragedy. (978-1-933110-99-8)

Heart 2 Heart by Julie Cannon. Suffering from a devastating personal loss, Kyle Bain meets Lane Connor, and the chance for happiness suddenly seems possible. (978-1-60282-000-5)

Queens of Tristaine by Cate Culpepper. When a deadly plague stalks the Amazons of Tristaine, two warrior lovers must return to the place of their nightmares to find a cure. (978-1-933110-97-4)

The Crown of Valencia by Catherine Friend. Ex-lovers can really mess up your life…even, as Kate discovers, if they've traveled back to the eleventh century! (978-1-933110-96-7)

Mine by Georgia Beers. What happens when you've already given your heart and love finds you again? Courtney McAllister is about to find out. (978-1-933110-95-0)

House of Clouds by KI Thompson. A sweeping saga of an impassioned romance between a Northern spy and a Southern sympathizer, set amidst the upheaval of a nation under siege. (978-1-933110-94-3)

Winds of Fortune by Radclyffe. Provincetown local Deo Camara agrees to rehab Dr. Bonita Burgoyne's historic home, but she never said anything about mending her heart. (978-1-933110-93-6)

Focus of Desire by Kim Baldwin. Isabel Sterling is surprised when she wins a photography contest, but no more than photographer Natasha Kashnikova. Their promo tour becomes a ticket to romance. (978-1-933110-92-9)

Blind Leap by Diane and Jacob Anderson-Minshall. A Golden Gate Bridge suicide becomes suspect when a filmmaker's camera shows a different story. Yoshi Yakamota and the Blind Eye Detective Agency uncover evidence that could be worth killing for. (978-1-933110-91-2)

Wall of Silence, 2nd ed. by Gabrielle Goldsby. Life takes a dangerous turn when jaded police detective Foster Everett meets Riley Medeiros, a woman who isn't afraid to discover the truth no matter the cost. (978-1-933110-90-5)

Mistress of the Runes by Andrews & Austin. Passion ignites between two women with ties to ancient secrets, contemporary mysteries, and a shared quest for the meaning of life. (978-1-933110-89-9)

Vulture's Kiss by Justine Saracen. Archeologist Valerie Foret, heir to a terrifying task, returns in a powerful desert adventure set in Egypt and Jerusalem. (978-1-933110-87-5)

Sheridan's Fate by Gun Brooke. A dynamic, erotic romance between physiotherapist Lark Mitchell and businesswoman Sheridan Ward set in the scorching hot days and humid, steamy nights of San Antonio. (978-1-933110-88-2)

Rising Storm by JLee Meyer. The sequel to *First Instinct* takes our heroines on a dangerous journey instead of the honeymoon they'd planned. (978-1-933110-86-8)

Not Single Enough by Grace Lennox. A funny, sexy modern romance about two lonely women who bond over the unexpected and fall in love along the way. (978-1-933110-85-1)

Such a Pretty Face by Gabrielle Goldsby. A sexy, sometimes humorous, sometimes biting contemporary romance that gently exposes the damage to heart and soul when we fail to look beneath the surface for what truly matters. (978-1-933110-84-4)

Second Season by Ali Vali. A romance set in New Orleans amidst betrayal, Hurricane Katrina, and the new beginnings hardship and heartbreak sometimes make possible. (978-1-933110-83-7)

Hearts Aflame by Ronica Black. A poignant, erotic romance between a hard-driving businesswoman and a solitary vet. Packed with adventure and set in the harsh beauty of the Arizona countryside. (978-1-933110-82-0)

Red Light by JD Glass. Tori forges her path as an EMT in the New York City 911 system while discovering what matters most to herself and the woman she loves. (978-1-933110-81-3)

Honor Under Siege by Radclyffe. Secret Service agent Cameron Roberts struggles to protect her lover while searching for a traitor who just may be another woman with a claim on her heart. (978-1-933110-80-6)

Dark Valentine by Jennifer Fulton. Danger and desire fuel a high-stakes cat-and-mouse game when an attorney and an endangered witness team up to thwart a killer. (978-1-933110-79-0)

Sequestered Hearts by Erin Dutton. A popular artist suddenly goes into seclusion, a reluctant reporter wants to know why, and a heart locked away yearns to be set free. (978-1-933110-78-3)

Erotic Interludes 5: Road Games, ed. by Radclyffe and Stacia Seaman. Adventure, "sport," and sex on the road—hot stories of travel adventures and games of seduction. (978-1-933110-77-6)

The Spanish Pearl by Catherine Friend. On a trip to Spain, Kate Vincent is accidentally transported back in time—an epic saga spiced with humor, lust, and danger. (978-1-933110-76-9)

Lady Knight by L-J Baker. Loyalty and honor clash with love and ambition in a medieval world of magic when female knight Riannon meets Lady Eleanor. (978-1-933110-75-2)

Dark Dreamer by Jennifer Fulton. Best-selling horror author Rowe Devlin falls under the spell of psychic Phoebe Temple. A Dark Vista romance. (978-1-933110-74-5)

Come and Get Me by Julie Cannon. Elliott Foster isn't used to pursuing women, but alluring attorney Lauren Collier makes her change her mind. (978-1-933110-73-8)

Blind Curves by Diane and Jacob Anderson-Minshall. Private eye Yoshi Yakamota comes to the aid of her ex-lover Velvet Erickson in the first Blind Eye mystery. (978-1-933110-72-1)

Dynasty of Rogues by Jane Fletcher. It's hate at first sight for Ranger Riki Sadiq and her new patrol corporal, Tanya Coppelli—except for their undeniable attraction. (978-1-933110-71-4)

Running With the Wind by Nell Stark. Sailing instructor Corrie Marsten has signed off on love until she meets Quinn Davies—one woman she can't ignore. (978-1-933110-70-7)